# CITY
# BEYOND
# TIME

# Books by John C. Wright

# CITY BEYOND TIME

## TALES OF THE FALL OF METACHRONOPOLIS

# JOHN C. WRIGHT

CASTALIA HOUSE

City Beyond Time: Tales of the Fall of Metachronopolis

John C. Wright

Published by Castalia House
Tampere, Finland
www.castaliahouse.com

Cover by Kirk DouPonce

ISBN: 978-952-7065-23-5

*History hath triumphed over time, which besides it nothing but eternity hath triumphed over.*

—Sir Walter Raleigh

# Contents

# Murder In Metachronopolis

## 16.

*Third beginning:*

I woke up when my gun jumped into my hand. It was an Unlimited Class Paradox Proctor Special, and it was better than any alarm, better than any guard dog.

I relaxed my eyelids open just a crack. It was dark. My balcony windows were fully polarized, so the glow from the golden towers outside showed only as faint, ghostly streaks reaching from pale mist below to black sky above.

The door, the creator, and the dreambox all showed like blocky shadows in the gloom. I couldn't see more. This was one of the rooms in a lower tower, a pretty shabby affair, not far above the mist, and the tower light from outside would have been dim even if the windows had been dialed to transparent.

There. A silhouette against the glass. It was tall, with some sort of wide headgear, perhaps with a plume above.

I raised my arm very slowly, careful not to rustle the sheets.

I said, in the Control language, "Lights!"

The lights came on.

He didn't look surprised. That is a bad sign.

The joker himself was dressed like a French Musketeer from Cardinal Richelieu's time, complete with ruffles, lace, tall boots, swordbelt, and pig-sticker. There was something about him that made me think he was real, not repro. Maybe it was the battered, used look of his hilt and scabbard; maybe it was the battered, used look of his face. Maybe it was the smell. Usually you can tell preindustrial from postindustrial types in one whiff.

One anachronism was the skullplug clinging like an insect to the base of his neck. And that was wrong, all wrong, if this guy was a party-killer. There are some strange types wandering like ghosts in the Towers, from every spot of history that ever was, and a lot that never were, drifting from party to party if they still got luster, or just drifting, if they don't. Some of the strangest are the party-killers, those who do murder just to see who is going to be resurrected by the next day, and who is forgotten.

But this guy was all wrong for that. Real party-killers never used brainjacks to record their sensations. For them, death had to be live, or else it was nothing.

Second, this guy didn't look nervous or scared. He had the not-surprised look of a bad actor going through a flat rehearsal.

Third, he recognized my piece. And not many people have seen the three-dimensional cross-section of an Unlimited Special. What I had in my hand wasn't the whole weapon array, arsenal, detection and tracking gear, etc. That would fill up a room, or even a warehouse. No, all I had in hand was the aiming-guide, the firing mechanisms, and the shielding unit which protected me from backscatter.

Still. Not many people know what it's like to look into the business end of an Unlimited Special. Not many at all.

"You're a Time Warden," I said.

"Very good, Mr. Frontino," he said. His voice was blurry and harsh, as if he were not used to using the vocal cords he was using now. "That is the quickest you've ever come to the correct conclusion—this time around."

"And you're going to pretend I don't remember the other versions, because of—why?"

He spread his hands awkwardly, a gesture like a puppet with a clumsy puppeteer would make. "That should be obvious, Mr. Frontino."

"My other versions are being killed. And I suppose that if I pulled this trigger, your alternates won't remember this version we're in now either, eh?"

"Unless they were monitoring, no. They say the only way to kill a Time Warden, a careful one who looks into his past and future, is to wait for him to kill himself. But you flatliners don't have that privilege, do you?" He smiled, sort of a sickly impersonation of good humor.

"Yeah. But we don't have to sneak around, so afraid of paradoxes that we can't even show our own faces in our own city that we allegedly rule. And we don't have groups of phonies and crazies out and about pretending that they're us when they're not."

I reached up with my other hand and made an adjustment. Dots from aiming lasers appeared on his groin and chest and the wrist of his right hand, which was a little too near the hilt of his sword for my taste.

(Think it's funny, a guy like me, armed as I was, afraid of his old-fashioned weapon, eh? People who think swords are quaint, not dangerous, never saw one used by a pro who knows his business. And the business is death by laceration, evisceration, impalement. No, swords are not quaint at all.)

I said: "There's one on the spot between your eyes, too. You can't see it."

"I'll take your word for it, Mr. Frontino."

I eyed him carefully up and down, looking for blurs or distortions which might indicate a timeshift. Nothing. Maybe he was actually all the way here, in this timespace, flying blind. But why? Most Time Wardens kept a version or two of themselves posted a minute or so in the future to give themselves plenty of warning for any surprises coming. Not him though. Why? Didn't make sense.

He was still waiting for my next line. He didn't just sit there and tell me what I was about to say, like most Time Wardens I'd met. Maybe he was less rude than most, or maybe he was just waiting for me to say something to let him know he was in the right version. Or, most likely, maybe he wasn't a Time Warden at all.

Whatever. "Spill it. Whatever you're here to say. Say it. Then get out."

"I'm here to hire you to solve a murder, Mr. Frontino."

"And you're pretending to be a Time Warden? Walk back into the past and look for yourself."

"It hasn't happened yet." Again, the crooked smile.

"Cute. And are you going to stop it if I solve it?"

"Not me. Not that I foresee." Again, the smile.

"Solve a crime and let it happen anyway, is that the plan? Sorry. Not interested. I'm retired. 'Bye."

"Retired? But aren't you the only Private Investigator in Metachronopolis? You've even got a fedora and a trenchcoat!"

"Everyone dressed like that when I'm from. And I'm retired as far as Time Wardens are concerned. Time Warden wants to solve a crime? Look it up in history book. Step into the past or future when its already been solved. What do you need mere mortals for? Manpower? Double yourself up a hundred times."

"There are limits to our powers. Grim limits. Though, sometimes, where exactly those boundaries lie are… misty."

He seemed to think that was funny. Before things got too humorous, I decided to cut things short. I opened the firing aperture with a twist of the wrist to maximum cone-of-blast and let him see me set the timer. The timer started beeping a countdown.

"I don't take cases from Time Wardens, see? All you guys are the same. The murderer turns out to be yourself, or you when you were younger. Or me. Or an alternate version of me, or you who turns out to be your own father fighting yourself for no reason except that is the way it was when the whole thing started. And there's no beginning and no reason for any of it. Oh, brother, you Time Wardens make me sick."

He drew himself up, all smiles gone now, all pretense at seeming human gone, too. My guess was it was not even his real body that he was wearing, just the corpse of some poor sap he murdered in order to have his personality jacked into the guy's brain. Perfect disguise. No fingerprints, no retina prints, no nothing. Just another flatliner dead for the convenience of the Time Wardens.

"Why did you retire from our service, Mr. Frontino?"

"Let's just say I was sick of cleaning up after all the messes you guys leave across all your pasts and futures. You'd think when you were done, you'd at least have the common decency to put everything back the way you found it."

"Everything? Absolutely everything?" His eyes were glittering now. "Be careful what you say, Mr. Frontino. Ideas have consequences."

The timer on my gun was entering its final cycle, chiming like a little tiny bit of Doomsday. "My friend here says you have about fifty seconds to leave. You have just enough time to try to scare me into taking the case by saying someone is knocking off these so-called 'other versions' of mine to stop me from taking it."

"No need for me to say it, Mr. Frontino. You're performing admirably."

"Forty seconds… Unless you want to admit you're not a Time Warden after all and tell me what this is really all about."

"No, Mr. Frontino. You will be convinced I am a Time Warden. And, before I forget to mention, you yourself will be the murder victim. I trust your interest in the case has increased? And should you still doubt my bona fides, here. I will leave a card."

And then he was gone. Something glittered in midair where he had been standing, the size of a playing card made of crystal, and fell with a chime of noise to my floor.

## 0.

Stories about Metachronopolis, the shining city outside of time, have many beginnings, they say. And I say that all come to the same miserable end. If you ask me. If there is anyone out there left to ask me.

## 29.

Let's start with the ending. I want you to imagine tumbling end over end in a featureless gray mist, no gravity, no nothing, watching in horror as your fingers dissolve.

You don't remember what this means or how you got here, of course, unless you've got special memory like mine. Hardened memory. A memory that remembers things that didn't happen, not in your timeline, anyway.

If you've got hardened memory, like mine, you can torment yourself to ease the boredom while you get erased, by going back over and over the stupid things you'd done, telling yourself that if you had the chance, just one more chance, you'd do it all differently next time around.

And if you're not too bright, it won't even occur to you that that's exactly the kind of thinking that got you into this mess in the first place.

(Except which place is the first place, anyway?)

## 1.

*First beginning:*

I regretted the words the moment I said them. But there are some things, once said, you can't take back.

I was opening my mouth to begin to apologize when she slapped my face. She leaned into the blow and gave me a good wallop, for a girl. Then she stood a moment, watching me with those beautiful hazel-gray eyes of hers. Beneath half-closed lids, her eyes were like sparks of luminous fire. She stood, lips pouted, one eyebrow arched, coldly studying the effect on me.

I raised my hand to rub my aching jaw. Maybe I didn't look sorry enough, or maybe I looked too sorry. Never can tell with women.

She turned on her heels and swayed over to the door. She gave me one last burning look over her shoulder.

"Babydoll, come back," I said. "I can make it right between us. Like none of that stuff ever happened. Like none of it ever had to happen…"

Maybe it sounded like I was whining, or maybe it sounded like I wasn't whining hard enough. Whatever, it was the wrong thing to say.

Disdain curled her perfect red lips. "You're a smart boy, Jake," she said, her voice husky and low and dripping with carefully chosen notes of contempt. "Smart enough to weasel out of some things. But not smart enough to know you can't weasel out of everything. Actions have consequences. Like this one. Watch me. Goodbye."

She swirled out the door, graceful as a lynx, and slammed it shut so sharply that the glass rattled. I saw her slim silhouette against the glass for a moment, and heard the bright clatter of her heels against the floorboards receding down the hallway toward the elevators.

Then she was gone.

## 17.

There wasn't any real government in this city, except for the hidden Time Wardens. But some of the important statesmen, Jefferson and Machiavelli and Caesar and a few guys like that, had thrown together a militia. Sometimes the militia circulated papers on unsavory characters, from petty thieves and party-crashers to the odd rapist or kidnapper who managed to get his hands on one of the famous women from history, Helen of Troy, or Cleopatra, that some of the Time Wardens kept around in their harems.

And then there was me. Why hadn't the Time Wardens shut me down long ago? No one knows why they do anything.

I pulled on my trousers and tucked in the tails of the shirt I hadn't bothered to take off when I sacked out on the couch. I whistled a command code toward the wardrobe and serving-beams draped my trenchcoat around my shoulders. Not that I expected to be cold in my own apartment; the fabric is woven with defensive webbing and detection-reaction cells. It's my own shabby version of a knight's shining armor.

Then the wardrobe slapped my hat onto my head. It must have thought that if I needed my coat, I needed my hat, right? Like I said, this was a low-tower apartment, and the circuits here were kind of dim.

I walked over slowly to where the Time Warden had been standing. Something was shining on the floor.

The card lay between my feet, glittering like a lake of deep ice. Distant shapes, like drowned buildings seen at the bottom of a clear lake, hovered in the cloudy reflection. I reached down...

### 18.

Perhaps I wasn't thinking. Perhaps it was what flatliners call a coincidence. Only I don't believe in coincidences. I know there are Time Wardens.

I had actually bent over and was reaching my hand down toward the damn thing when my smartgun emitted its shrieking chronodistortion alarm. It jumped out of its holster and into my hand. The grip tingled where the energy field had to grab my fingers and fold them around the stock.

By then it was too late. My eyes had focused on the image floating deep below the mirrored surface of the card. This one was attention-activated.

Whenever a human brain pays attention to any event, the possible timelines radiating from that point multiply, since that observation affects the human's actions. There are circuits that can detect these multiplications, though I'd never heard of one being focused through a destiny card.

You look. You're trapped. Very neat, very tidy.

It was a picture of a wide, high place surrounded by pillars. Of course I recognized it. The Pyrtaneum of the Time Wardens. And then I was there.

## 19.

"Welcome to the crime scene, Mr. Frontino."

## 3.

*Second beginning. This one brighter than the others:*

I recall my first view of the city.

I thought it was a job interview. I had no other work, no future, and the best woman I had ever laid eyes on walked out on me the night before. I wasn't in a great mood, but, at that point, I was willing to listen to anything.

Almost anything.

"Time travelers?" I said, trying to look chipper. I was trying to think of a polite way to say goodbye and get lost.

He didn't look crazy. (The real crazies never do). Mr. Iapetus was a foreign-looking fellow in a long red coat of a fabric I didn't recognize. He had dark, magnetic eyes, high cheekbones, and wore a narrow goatee.

His office was appointed with severe and restrained elegance. To one side, a row of dark bookshelves loomed; in the center was a wide mahogany desk, polished surface gleaming; to the other side, heavy drapes blocked a hidden length of window. I did not think it odd at the time to see bright sunlight shining from the carpet at the lower hem of the window drapes. But it had been raining outside when I entered the lobby just behind me.

Mr. Iapetus was standing by the window. He took up a fold of drapes in his hand. "I believe in what you might call the shock therapy method of indoctrination. It helps make the tedious period of disbelief more brief."

A wide yank of his arm threw the drapes aside. A spill of blinding sunlight washed around me.

Blinking, I saw I was high up, overlooking a shining city. I had been on the ground floor when I came in. Now, I was miles up in the air. And glory was underfoot.

### 4.

"Behold Metachronopolis, the city beyond the reach of time!"

Towers made of gleaming gold, taller than tall mountains, rose in streamlined ramparts all around me, like swords held up in high salute. Far underfoot, in the canyons and gulfs between the towers, cloudbanks drifted, stained cerise and gold from the light shed by the towers.

Great bridges, elfin-graceful, arched across the miles from balcony to balcony of the gleaming structures, with giant statues placed at even intervals, sentry-like, along their tremendous length. The balconies were thickly grown with hedges and arbors, and the bridges were like parklands suspended in the air, with figures dimly glimpsed strolling among the greenery. Or flying.

I thought they were seagulls at first. They rose from the clouds below. Bright figures rose and soared past the window, comet-swift, and I saw that they were manlike beings, robed in cloaks of light which fanned out like angel wings to either side of them. Up along the wind they fled, swifter than rising sparks, handsome men, and women with faces like young girls, heads thrown back and eyes alit with pleasure. They were dressed in the costumes of all ages.

Among the flock were monsters and animal-headed people, like the gods of ancient Egypt, jackal-headed or hawk-headed, like satyrs and chimera.

The air was alive with fliers, darting from window to window, or from minaret to minaret, balcony to balcony, bridge to rooftop garden.

And, dimly through the glass, I heard the air was filled with music.

Iapetus' voice rang with pride: "Many histories have many strange beginnings, but time travel is inevitable in every time line, and, from time travelers, Time Wardens grow, and all come here, their mighty monuments and towers to build. Yes! Metachronopolis has many beginnings, but all timelines lead to her!"

I was impressed by the sights. "When do I get my chance to sign up?" I said softly.

Iapetus opened the window. I smelled the scent of wind-blown petals on the far gardens, and heard the flourish of trumpets, and the tolling of deep bells. "In a sense," he said, "You already have. Examine your memory."

He took a gun out of his pocket and shot me in the leg. I fell screaming, blood pumping through the fingers I clenched onto my shattered knee...

And then he hadn't. Never had. No gun, no wound.

The shocking memory of having been shot, horribly wounded, was already beginning to fade, like a bad dream.

But I didn't let it fade. For one thing, it was impossible for me to have two separate and distinct, mutually contradictory memories of the same event.

For another, I wanted to remember the look on Iapetus' face as he shot. Just for a second, as he raised the strange pistol, he wore a look so inhuman and expressionless, that I would have called it cruel, if he hadn't seemed so cavalier and nonchalant...

"Deja Vu is a milder form of the same phenomenon," he continued in the same bored, dry tone. "Some people have a naturally hardened memory. Our training can increase the talent. A talent utterly useless except when there is a Time Warden nearby, manipulating the chronocosm. Then it is precious. Useful to us. Our instruments show you have a strong natural hardness of memory; a stubborn streak. Being able to remember alternate versions after a change does not make you a Time Warden, of course. But, still, it's better than being a flatliner. We call it pawn memory. I trust you see the humor? Pawns cannot leave their own files, their own timelines, so to speak, unless a major piece is near. And, yes, some pawns reach the final row."

I was not sure I liked the idea of being anyone's pawn. But then I wondered what this final row might look like.

## 20.

So of course I recognized the place. Highest tower in the city, biggest, brightest. A vast floor of shining black marble, inset with panels of mirrored destiny crystal, stretched across acres toward wide balconies, which looked down upon the titanic gold towers far below. The place looked like it was open to the air on every side, but between the tall pillars there must have been panes of invisible glass or some sort of force field to maintain the pressure at this altitude. The sky above was so dark blue it was almost black.

I think I saw the curve of the horizon.

Standing near one of the thrones that formed a semicircle embracing the floor, was D'Artagnan. Standing near me was a cataphract in power armor, circa A.D. 4400, the era of the Machine Wars. The cataphract had his faceplate up, and I could see the cold, no-nonsense look in his eye. His armor was throbbing on stand-by; I could hear the idling hum of the disrupter grids and the clicking of the launch-pack warm-up check from here.

There was a whine from his elbow servo-motors when he folded his arms, putting his fingers near the control points on his chestplate.

I was fast with my smartgun. I didn't think I was that fast. I put it back in the holster, slowly, like a nice little boy who didn't want to get flattened.

At his nod, an aiming monocle clicked out of its slot on his helmet visor and fell over his eye. Little red dots danced up and down upon my chest, just to let me know he was thinking of me.

I turned to D'Artagnan. "Cute trick with the destiny card," I said.

"You didn't want to be here. Well, now you are."

"What's the big idea with the tin can here?" I said, hooking a thumb at the cataphract.

"That should be obvious, Mr. Frontino. We want you to solve a murder, not to prevent it. Even highly trained paradox proctors get uncertain about their oaths if ever they look into the circumstances of their own future deaths. They always wonder, can't the universe stand just one more small strain? Surely one more tiny fold in the fabric of time won't unravel the whole web? And what does it matter to me anyway, if the chronocosm dies, so long as I myself survive?"

He chuckled, then added: "If that's what loyal knot-cutters think, well, what are we to expect from one who is retired? Especially since he did not ask our permission to retire, did he?"

I turned away. I wasn't sure what I would say, so all I did say was: "And where's the body?"

"I have composed a null-time vacuole to bracket the event," he said, drawing a mirrored destiny card from his doublet. "You may examine it at your leisure."

First clue: why was D'Artagnan bothering to say so much here? Time Wardens are only talkative in virgin time. When they've been through the same scene a dozen times or so, they usually get right to the point. He had been acting the same way last night, when he interrupted my beauty sleep. Was there such a thing as a Time Warden who didn't like to time travel?

Clue two: why me? Why these high-pressure tactics to herd me into this thing? They had other paradox-killers. Plenty. One of them was looming behind me right now, dressed in his happy mechanical-man suit.

D'Artagnan slid the destiny card into the crystal material of the nearest throne arm. The throne itself was made of a block of the same "substance" as the card: an area of frozen time-energy. (I've always wondered why they make their chairs that way. I guess nothing else is good enough for a Time Warden to warm his butt on. On the other hand, no one could monkey around with any of these throne's histories, not made of what they were, or go back and have had built bombs or bugging cells inside them or other nasty gimmicks.)

And the strip of the floor leading from the throne to where I was standing was also made of the same substance. I imagined the new scene too clearly to deny it. And I was there.

## 21.

I imagined a single, still moment of time.

Everything was "lit" by the weird non-glow of null-time. Any object grew bluer and dimmer the longer you stared at it. I was used to the effect; I kept my gaze swinging back and forth as I stepped into the scene, always moving. D'Artagnan and the cataphract stepped in behind me, the motorized legs on the power-armor humming with understated strength.

There were only two figures frozen in the moment of the murder scene. One was motionless on a throne, armored in ice and cloaked in mist; his face, a mirror. The other was a tall guy, not so good-looking, trenchcoat scarlet with motionless flame, stylish fedora suspended in mid-air to one side of his head. He was in the middle of getting shot, impaled on an energy-blast.

Yours truly. Of course. And to think that one of my goals in life had been to leave a good looking corpse.

I looked at the blast first.

It originated off to the left. Near one of the pillars, about shoulder-high, a small puff of mist was frozen. Trailing out from it, motionless, like a worm made of flame, was a line of Cherenkov radiation, and knots and streamers of cloud where the atmosphere couldn't get out of the way fast enough to avoid being vaporized. Little glowing balls like St. Elmo's fire dotted the fiery discharge-stream, where ionized oxygen molecules were being turned into ozone. An even brighter crooked line paralleling the discharge-path indicated where atoms had been split by the force of the passing bullet.

At the other end of the discharge-stream was me, also ending. I looked at myself hanging in mid-air, caught in mid-explosion and mid-death. My smartgun was leaping like a salmon trying, too late, to get into my fingers. It hung, frozen, a few inches above my out-flung hand. Not smart enough this time, it seemed.

I (the me version of me, that is) stepped through clouds of blood and flying steam to get a closer look at me (the becoming-a-corpse version of me). The exit wound was enormous, as if half my chest and all of my left arm had been drawn in hazy red chalk-smudges by an Impressionist artist.

The smell was terrible. I know the textbooks say you're not supposed to be able to smell anything in null-time. But, I figure, if my eye can move through a cloud of frozen photons and pick up an image, then my nose can move through a nimbus of blood-cloud and sniff roasted flesh.

There was no visible entry wound. Of course. The bullet must have been ultra-microscopic, perhaps only a few molecules wide, in order to be small enough to slip through my smartgun's watchdog web. And it must have been traveling fast enough, a hefty percentage of the speed of light, to be quick enough to get me before my smartgun could react.

And the bullet was programmed, somehow, to drop velocity and transfer its kinetic energy to my body in a broad, slow shockwave as it struck.

Somehow? A time-retardation wave could do it. The relative velocity would change once it left the field. Just another application of the same technology which made my smartgun.

Heck. I could have this done this myself, with a smartgun just like the one I had. I already thought of two different ways to reproduce this effect just with the programs I presently had loaded.

I straightened up and backed away, brushing anachronistic drops of blood off my coat.


### 23.

After I was done looking at the figure on the throne, I turned and addressed D'Artagnan. "I need to take a reading of the time depth and energy signature of the discharge wave with the sensors in my smartgun. I'm going to draw it nice and slow, so your steel gorilla knows I'm on the level here. That all right with you?"

D'Artagnan spread his hands. "That's fine."

For the first time, I noticed a slight blur of mist around his fingers as he made the gesture.

He had time-doubled. It looked like a Recursive Alternate Information shift, but I wasn't sure. There was an alternate line out there somewhere where he had done something else with his hand. Maybe he had touched a control or given a hand signal to the cataphract. Or, if it was actually a Recursive Anachronism shift, he might have handed something forward or backward to himself.

Or he might not have done anything at all. With a Parallel Displacement shift, a Time Warden, standing a few seconds away, pacing us, could have handed him something.

I drew my smartgun slowly.


## 25.

And I was thinking: Why not?

Why the hell not? Hitler's mother-to-be, Klara, age sixteen, looked up at me with eyes as wide and trusting and innocent and hurt as any you'd ever dream of seeing. She hadn't done anything wrong. Maybe she would have said something, but the slug had torn out her throat. She got blood all over my pants and shoes when she fell toward me. It had smelled then much the way it smelled now.

Stalin's mother, Ketevan Geladze, on the other hand, was already pregnant, a pretty blond with a cheerful smile and coke-bottle-bottom-thick eyeglasses, when the Time Wardens decided to abort her future. They had me shoot her in the stomach twice more after she fell, burnt and screaming, just to make sure her helpless baby would be dead.

Why not? They can all make it undone again. Or so they told me.

And then one Time Warden or another took a dislike to the atomic wars of the 2020's. Einstein was a little boy playing with mud-pies in a backyard garden when my misplaced scattershot tore off his arms and legs and left him blind, bleeding, and screaming in pain until I could reprogram and fire a particle beam to put him out of his misery.

When I asked to be allowed to go back and do that assassination again, maybe cleaner, the Time Warden's representative told me that chronoportation should not be used for frivolous reasons. He sternly warned me that paradox weakened the fabric of timespace.

Why not?

I won't even tell you who I had to kill to let a curious Time Warden explore the alternate line where Christianity never rose to dominance in Europe. At least that one was done with a clean shot to the head.

Why not?

If I could set out to kill pregnant women and innocent girls and little boys and the nicest guy I'd ever met, why not set out to kill me?

### 22.

I looked around to see who I had been (was going to be) talking to, when I was (would be) shot.

Only one of the thrones was occupied. There he was in all his regalia. A Time Warden. His armor was made, not of metal, but of destiny crystal, gleaming like ice. From his shoulders depended a cloak of mist, created from a single thread vibrating backward and forward across several seconds. The cloak of distorted time fell from his shoulders in streamers of vapor, dripped across and down the chair arms where he sat, and hovered in curls around his ankles.

I could not see his face. His crown was projecting a forcefield like a mirrored helmet to protect his head from the radiation of the murderous discharge in front of him.

Clue three: why did the Time Warden's armor have time to react to the assassin's bolt when the victim's smartgun did not? Coincidence? But I didn't believe in coincidences. What people call coincidences are sloppy, makeshift arrangements by the Time Wardens to put frayed or broken timelines back on track.

And I sure as hell didn't believe in Time Wardens any more.

## 5.

Iapetus leaned past me and opened the window. He paused a moment, allowing me to savor the smell of the high gardens, the deep chime of distant bells, to hear the calls and cries of delight from the winged fliers.

He spoke: "There need be no further interview nor testing. Any Time Warden dissatisfied with your future performance would have already retroactively informed me. The choice is now yours."

He straightened his back and looked at me. "The rewards of loyal service to the Time Wardens are many…"

## 1(a).

This time around, I didn't say anything to her. I bit back the angry confession which sprang to my lips. There are some things which, once said, can never be taken back.

Instead, I put my hands on her shoulders, and drew her closer. "Babydoll, there's no other woman. There is no one else…" I lied smoothly.

This time, my past didn't catch up with me. I could always outrun it, always stay one jump ahead of the game. I smothered the pang of guilt I felt at the thought as I lowered my head to kiss her.

## 6.

"…including material rewards, without limit…"

## 10.

While I was waiting for the croupier, and the manager, and the manager's assistant, to collect my winnings into a large suitcase, I stepped into a telephone booth, with a copy of tomorrow's stock market under my arm, to make a call to my broker.

I yawned while the phone rang. It all seemed so tedious, so safe. Maybe this time around I would walk into the ambush the thugs hired by the manager were planning.

## 7.

"...as well as the knowledge that you are doing good and useful work to preserve both past historic treasures and the integrity of the timespace continuum..."

## 11.

The Roman legionary stood there, shaking and sweating, eyes rolling wildly, unable to move, locked in the grip of my paralysis ray. I would have preferred to shoot him, of course, but orders were not to chance future archeologists puzzling over slugs found in one of Caesar's troopers. I could tell the Roman wanted to scream when I pulled his short sword from its scabbard, put the point under the belt of his armor, and pushed.

He fell down the steps of the Library at Alexandria, and I kicked the torch he'd been holding down after him, safely away from the precious scrolls and papyrus.

There was blood splashed all over my coat and trousers.

I was doing good work. Important work. Why did it make me feel sick to my stomach?

A whole squad of legionaries led by a centurion trotted around the corner at a quickstep, shields and pilum in hand. They let out a roar when they saw their dead comrade, and shouted vows of vengeance to their gods. Then they lowered spears, formed ranks, and charged the stairs.

I laughed. Did they expect me to wait around for their vengeance? For the consequences of my actions to catch up with me? They would never catch up.

A twist on the barrel of my smartgun opened the paralysis induction beam to wide-fan. The soldiers fell, and then they waited, helplessly, for me to slaughter them. I tried not to look them in the eyes as I moved from one to the next with their comrade's gladius in my hand.

## 8.

"...and, since the Time Wardens are all-powerful, no one can oppose them or stop them. They have no enemies..."

## 13.

When I woke up, I found myself slumped in a heavy, high-backed chair of dark red leather, placed at the end of a long conference table of black walnut. Nine hooded figures sat around the length of the table.

Light came from two high candelabrums, burning real candles and dripping messy wax onto the table surface. The room around me was dim; I had the impression we were in a library. There were no windows, no clocks, nothing like a calendar anywhere in sight. I could hear no noise from outside. It may have been day or night, of any season, of any year.

The robes, likewise, could have been from practically any date or era. They all wore gloves; I saw no rings or jewelry.

"Do not be alarmed," came a polite tenor from my left. "I know you do not recall this, but you volunteered to have a small part of your recent memory blotted out. It was a condition our anonymity required to make this conversation possible. You wanted to speak with us."

"And who are you supposed to be?" I asked, straightening up, my fingers pressed against my throbbing temples. "And why the hell did I—you claim—want to speak to you so badly?"

The hooded figure at the other end of the table leaned forward slightly. He had a rumbling, bass voice. "We are the enemies of the Time Wardens, Mr. Frontino…"

## 24.

I drew my smartgun slowly, so as not to startle D'Artagnan or Ugly Boy in the fancy steel suit. Idiots. They might have stood a chance if Ugly Boy had had enough sense to keep his faceplate down. As it was, I gyro-focused an aiming laser to keep a dot right between his eyes where he couldn't see it, while taking a reading on the energy discharge which killed (was going to kill) me (future-me). I didn't have to actually point the gun barrel at Ugly Boy to shoot him; my gun was pretty damn smart.

The formation readings did not surprise me. The energy signature was exactly the same as that generated by the gun held in my hand. It was not the same make or model, it was the exact same gun.

Of course. Obviously. I was going to shoot myself.

Means I could see. What about opportunity?

The time-depth reading on the spot of mist from which the murder-discharge radiated did surprise me. It was a matter of a few seconds, plus or minus. Something was going to make me shoot me in a moment or so from now.

That left only motive. And I couldn't imagine any motive, at first. But then I thought: Why not? Why the hell not?

### 26.

I swung my barrel to cover D'Artagnan.

"OK, fancy boy," I snapped. "Charade's over. Do I need to shoot you to make the real Time Warden show up?"

"You think I am not a Time Warden?"

I shook my head. I could have explained that I hadn't seen him chronoshift but once, and that, since he wasn't wearing a Time Warden's mist cloak, such shifts would have been obvious. A Time Warden who did not have other selves as bodyguards? Who lived through all his time lines in blind, first-time, unedited scenes? A Time Warden who didn't time travel? But all I said was: "You talk too much to be a Time Warden."

"You may as well put your gun away, Mr. Frontino, or I will have my..." he nodded toward the cataphract and his sentence choked to a halt. He saw the aiming dot punctuating Ugly Boy's face.

"I don't know if you can see my settings from there," I said.

He nodded carefully. "Your deadman switch is on."

"And the change-in-energy detector. Any weapons go off near me, and my Unlimited friend here goes off and keeps going off long after I'm dead. Well? Well? I want some answers!"

The cataphract's launch-harness unfolded from his back like the legs of a preying mantis opening. Tubes longer than bazookas pointed at me. He raised his hand toward me. With sharp metallic clashes of noise, barrels came out of the weapon housings of his gauntleted forearms. I was standing close enough that I could hear the throbbing hum of his power-core cycling up to full-battle mode.

The mouths of his weapons were so close to my face that I could smell ozone and hot metal.

My nape hairs and armpits prickled. I could feel my heartbeat pulsing in my temples; my face felt hot. Standing at ground zero, at the point-blank firing focus of a mobile Heavy Assault Battery, really doesn't do a man's nerves much good.

"Well?" I said, not taking my eyes from D'Artagnan. "Things are going to start getting sloppy!"

Even D'Artagnan looked surprised when the frozen image of the Time Warden on the throne stood up and raised his hand. Of course the time-stop had meant nothing to him. He had merely been sitting still, faking it.

"Enough!" His voice rang with multiple echoes, as if a crowd of people were speaking in not-quite-perfect unison. "You have passed our test, Frontino. You were brought here to assume the rights, powers and perquisites of a Time Warden. You may assume your rightful place at my side. There is no need for a coronation ceremony. Here I give the reality of power."

With a casual flick of his wrist, he tossed a packet of destiny cards at my feet. The pack fell open as it struck the marble floor. Shining mirrored cards fell open, glittering.

These were the real things. The glassy depths held images from history, ages past and future, eras unguessed. There were castles, landscapes, battlefields, towers, all the cities and kingdoms of the world.

The final row lay before me. All I had to do was stoop over and pick them up. If I just bent a little, it could all be mine. Me, pulling the strings for once. Me, the puppet-master, not the puppet. No longer a pawn.

## 9.

I stood at the window, watching the golden city of glory with eyes of awe. I asked Iapetus. "I still have some questions. May I ask?"

"Certainly, Mr. Frontino."

"How can it be possible? Time travel, I mean? What happens to cause-and-effect?"

Iapetus' smile was sinister and cold. "Cause-and-effect is a delusion of little minds. A cultural prejudice. The ancient wisdom of the prescientific ages recognized that the workings of the universe were held in the hands of unguessable powers. They called them gods instead of Time Wardens. But it is all one."

I asked: "So what happens if you kill your grandfather?"

"Nothing truly exists," explained Iapetus impatiently. "Except as a range of uncertain probabilities. Normally this uncertainty is confined to the sub-atomic level, creating the illusions of solid matter, life, and causality.

"If you killed a remote ancestor," he continued, "The uncertainty of the events springing from that would increase, since your likelihood of existing in your present constitution would decrease. You might possibly survive having a remote ancestor killed; there is a small chance that some of your genes and elements might pop into existence without any cause. Certain sub-atomic particles do so, although it is unlikely that trillions of particles would leap together spontaneously to form you, but it might happen. Killing your father is remotely unlikely, however, as the uncertainty involved would become macroscopic. Visible to the naked eye."

"Visible as what?"

"Mist. Photons bouncing from you become randomized in their paths as your exact position becomes uncertain. It looks like a blur of mist stretching between the various points you might affect. Gravitons likewise become uncertain, and the Earth no longer attracts all of your mass."

But then he smiled and made a casual gesture. "But why dwell on such an ending? Rest assured that if there is any possible timeline which avoids such an appalling end, the Time Wardens will shunt you into it."

"But won't that shunt itself create more uncertainty? Another paradox?"

"Perhaps," he said with an airy wave of his hand and a snort of disdain. "But why worry? The results of that paradox can be postponed by means of additional paradoxes."

"Doesn't sound quite right," I said. "Like borrowing on credit to pay off bad credit. What happens tomorrow, when all the bills come due? What happens when the loan shark comes to collect? There is always a loan shark."

"For a time traveler, tomorrow does not exist unless he chooses to walk into it. And, if you are loyal to the Time Wardens, you may, one day, be exalted to that high position yourself, and have all the past and future as your plaything. Well? What do you say?"

## 27.

The cards lay shining at my feet on the marble floor.

"Well?" came the many voices of the single Time Warden. "What do you say?"

## 14.

"Am I supposed to be impressed?" I asked the hooded figures seating around the dark table. "So you are the famous enemies of the Time Wardens. Anachronists! The Anarchists of Time! But, really, how can you even exist?"

I glared at them. A faceless bunch of black hoods stared back. In the dark alleys and darker rooms of the lower towers, you hear rumors about Anachronists. Back when I was working on the Helen of Troy case, I even met a guy who said he'd met one, or was one, or something.

"How can you fight them?" I continued. I did not bother to keep the scorn out of my voice. "Use time travel? Then you are Time Wardens yourselves, whether you admit it or not. And if you don't or can't time travel, you're sunk!"

"We are their enemies, but they are not ours. We are in nowise Anarchists of Time. This is but their name for us," said the deep bass voice. "Our loyalty is not to time at all. We are the Servants of Eternity."

"Don't dodge the question. How do you fight them?"

"Simple. We do not. Why bother? Time Wardens are creatures of unreason. They deny cause and effect; they act without heed for the consequences of their actions. We need only stand by while they destroy themselves. The only thing we really need to do is warn their victims before they too fall into the same trap."

"Which victims?"

"You, for one, Mr. Frontino. Drug users often become drug pushers to afford their habit. Likewise, time paradox patrolmen must often become Time Wardens to protect their own personal past from being snarled or destroyed by Time Wardens."

"Me? A Time Warden? They're going to make me one?"

"Perhaps someday."

"And *that* is what you want to protect me from?" I had to laugh. "Why not 'protect me' from becoming a millionaire? Why not 'protect me' from becoming a god?"

The tenor voice from the left spoke. "Say, rather, we want to protect you from playing at God. Don't you recognize that time travel, by its very nature, is, and must be, immoral? That it is, and must be, insane?"

I stood up. "Very dramatic. Look, I don't know what kind of crackpots you are, but if it comes down to a showdown between you bunch of flatliners and the Time Wardens, I think I want to be on the winning side, thank you. So where's the exit to this madhouse, eh?"

I slid my hand into my coat as I stood. I was expecting my shoulder-holster to be empty. Instead, my fingers closed around the streamlined grip of my smartgun with a familiar magnetic tingle. I felt warmth in my palm. The circuits were active.

That stumped me. Why the hell would the self-proclaimed enemies of the Time Wardens let me go fully armed in their midst? One of the robed figure spread his gloves, and spoke in a light, soft voice. Maybe it was a her. "Please, Mr. Frontino. Allow us a moment to explain ourselves. Perhaps we strike you as zealous. That does not necessarily mean that our conclusions are wrong, does it? Let us have our say, then you can judge for yourself. Your powers of reasoning are good. Use them."

This had not been the way Lord Iapetus had spoken, back when I had been first recruited. I sat.

The one at the head of the table—the bass voice—spoke: "Time travel (and I do not include harmless sight-seeing) means using future knowledge to change the past. It means an attempt to elude the consequences of reality, without caring whether or not you cause the paradoxes that will someday destroy reality. Time travel and morality cannot co-exist. Morality judges the goodness of acts by their intentions and consequences. Time travelers deny consequences are related to intentions, or even that consequences exist at all. Is it right to kill an innocent young girl who will one day become Adolf Hitler's mother? Be careful before you answer. You yourself do not know what tyrants you may some day father, Mr. Frontino. Or become."

"Maybe it's not so moral," I said. "But so what? Flatliners can't fight Time Wardens. They're all-powerful."

There was a murmur of laughter around the room at that. One amused voice said: "All-powerful? They are as helpless as condemned criminals on death row. The Time Wardens are living on borrowed

time. They know it. Don't you? You've seen what's at the bottom
of their towers, haven't you? Tell us, Mr. Frontino, what is at the
foundation of the city of Metachronopolis?"

## 12.

Some Time Warden or another wanted to reward my squad for the
work we had done destroying the technological progress of civilization circa A.D. 2300. It had been a delicate bit of work, since we had
to eliminate the society's ability to investigate temporal mechanics—
can't have a bunch of flatliners developing time travel on their own,
after all—without eliminating the technological progress leading to
the development of some of the Time Warden's favorite toys from
later eras—including the multidimensional matrix formulations involved in smartguns like mine or cataphract-style armor.

But we had done well, killing all the right people at the right time,
and the Time Warden invited us to his tower for a party. Everyone
who still had luster to him was there then, including a dozen versions
of Keats, each reading a slightly different variation of his completed
poem, *Hyperion*, and an older and a younger version of Agamemnon,
who some Time Warden had brought as a joke in order to watch
the older version trying to convince his younger self not to go to
Troy. There was also a confused version of Thomas Jefferson who
was talking to descendants of Shaka Zulu from an obscure timeline
where blacks kept whites as plantation slaves in Virginia. Richard
the Lionheart and Saladin had been given antigravitic power-armor,
and were flying around the party scene, blowing huge chunks in the
scenery and unwary guests while trying to get each other. All great
fun.

I kept noticing the servants. There were so many people who lived
among these towers whose memories were not hardened enough to
remember who they were or where they came from. People who

had been forgotten by the Time Wardens once they were no longer amusing. Young versions of Cleopatra and Semiramis were both working that evening as cocktail waitresses, trying to earn enough money to keep their rooms in the lower towers. In other worlds, they had once been queens, but their eras were apparently no longer in style among the Time Wardens. They were no longer invited to parties or functions, but they knew too much about the future to be allowed back home. I saw a Cleopatra serving a drink to a Julius Caesar who either came from a timeline where he'd never met her or was just a jerk who pretended he didn't recognize her. Sad.

Since she lived in a bad section of the towers, I walked that Cleo home after the main part of the party was over (more famous parties became part of the Time Wardens' Eternal Circuit, and never ended). Seeing how dark and misty things were at these depths, and since I still had the security all-pass which had gotten me into the Time Warden's tower to begin with, I wondered if I could get past the lower areas and see what was at the bottom of these towers. From the sounds which sometimes came up from below, I had to wonder. I knew it was forbidden, but I was in a pretty dour mood and didn't much give a damn anyway, so...

## 15.

In a queasy voice, I answered the Enemies of the Time Wardens. "Mist. Mist and uncertainty. There is no bottom. It just gets more and more misty the further down you go..."

I shivered at the memory. The lower bridge had been invisible beneath my feet, swaying, soft and marshy, mutating in shape even as I walked. The gargoyle looming on the railing beside me had worn one face, then, after the mists blurred past, another. It had been dark, with muddled images of tower-roots fading and swaying around me. The thick tower walls were nothing but streams of smoke. From the abyss underfoot, a screaming voice begged me not to pick up the white cards. I shouted back, but there had been no answer...

"The towers don't have any foundations," I said.

More laughter. A young man's voice came cheerfully from the right, "An apt metaphor for the Time Wardens' whole system of thought, I deem."

This laughing all the time was beginning to get on my nerves. Maybe because I had almost never heard a Time Warden laugh. Not nice laughter, anyway.

"What do you guys want from me?" I demanded.

"We would like you to withdraw your loyalty from the Time Wardens, not just the present group, but from the whole concept of time travel; to avoid time travel as much as possible; to prepare your memory for a massive shock. Major timeline changes are due once the Time Wardens are overthrown."

"You are talking about the elimination of time travel altogether?"

"Is there any other position we can take, given our philosophy?"

"Eliminate how?"

"By letting nature take its course."

"You talk as if it is... inevitable."

The robed figure shrugged and spread his gloves. "Suppose you are a Time Warden, Mr. Frontino. Another Time Warden has gone back do something which might affect your past, something that may alter the circumstances of your culture and history, or even eliminate your birth. Whether his meddling is deliberate or not, what is the safest way to neutralize his interference? Safest, quickest, best?"

That was an easy one. How did Time Wardens solve all their problems? "Eliminate him."

"Just him? Remember that you cannot reason with the other Time Wardens. If they were people who listened to warnings about the consequences of their actions, they would not be time travelers in the first place."

"If time travel necessarily—you claim—and inevitably—you claim —eliminates whoever does it," I said, "Then what happens after everything collapses?"

The bass voice said: "Our research indicates that there is one core timeline, the line where time travel was never invented. The whole unwieldy structure of multiple branching time lines and time loops manipulated by the lords of Metachronopolis is a temporary shadow or reflection of that core line into the surrounding chronic ylem. Our chronocosm is temporary and unstable, like the creation of certain virtual particle pairs in base vacuum, which exist for a brief time before they eliminate themselves. But some of us remember the core line. Surely you recall what your life was like before you meddled with time travel."

I shrugged. "My life wasn't so great."

"But better than this."

I shook my head. "I don't need to listen to any more of this. Look, your whole argument is based on the idea that Time Wardens are all some sort of criminals or infantile maniacs. You're basically saying that they will keep meddling and monkeying with the past until they eliminate themselves. I don't buy it. Aren't some of them reasonable? Don't some of them listen to reason?"

"That is always our hope, Mr. Frontino. We would not bother talking to you if we did not have that hope. Here."

There was a mirrored glitter as he took a card from his robe. Then, with a flick of his gloved fingers, he slid it across the table toward me.

I did not reach for it. "What is this supposed to be?"

"Think of it as the Final Destiny crystal. It is a destiny card attached to the core line. Naturally, you can only use it once. Once you are in the core line, time travel is impossible, and you cannot come out."

I looked down.

The surface of the card was completely black, with no image at all inside of it.

It might have been my imagination, but I thought I felt a sensation of immense cold radiating from the dead-black surface.

"No thanks," I said, leaning slightly backward from the absolutely featureless, dark card. "Go back to being a flatliner with a blind future and irrevocable past? Sorry. Let me out of here. Unless you got something more for me to hear?"

They didn't.

One of them—I think it was a woman—got up and held a candle near a mirrored frame on the far wall. Except it wasn't a mirror; inside the depth, I saw a picture of one of the bridge-top wintergardens near the Museum of Man, high up near the center of the city, shining with golden towers. The picture surged into my imagination…

Another question occurred to me, and so I turned around, but there was only a golden bridge-way behind me. The Anachronists were gone.

### 28.

"Where are the other Time Wardens?" I asked the mirrored figure on the throne. "Or is elevating me to Wardenship just something you decided all on your lonesome?"

An eerie, bubbling noise like many disjointed voices laughing came from the mirrored mask. "Other Time Wardens? Why should there be *other* Time Wardens? How would you expect us to govern ourselves?"

That one stumped me. I squinted. "Don't know. I always thought you guys had a leader, or you took a vote or something…"

Again, I heard the weird blurred laughter. "Why should I tolerate to abide by the outcome of any vote, when I could play the scene again and again until the vote came out as I desired? How much less would I brook the commands of a leader! Why should I tolerate any difference of opinion of any kind whatsoever! If I know a man's birthdate, or his mother's, then he exists at my sufferance only for so long as it should please me!"

"Yeah, right. What are these other thrones for, then?"

"They are meant for the other versions of me!"

"Pretty empty now, aren't they?"

A terrible silence hung in the air.

I said slowly, "You're becoming more and more unlikely now, aren't you? There are fewer and fewer alternates because you've eliminated the other possibilities. You've mucked around in the past so much that you've edited yourself out of the cosmos, haven't you? And you couldn't stop meddling in history, even when you knew it was destroying you…"

"You will meddle when you become a Time Warden also. It is our nature. Pick up the cards, brother Time Warden. I command it."

"And if I say no?"

His stood up, his cloak of mist writhing and billowing around his glinting mirrored armor as he stood. The voices from the mask were blurrier now, shouting: "Then you will die!"

I don't know who fired first, me or the cataphract. The Time Warden threw his mist-cloak up, so that my shots and lines of hissing energy went into the mist, became uncertain, and vanished before they even reached the Time Warden.

Without thinking, I switched to a special program, something small enough and fast enough—a few molecules wide, accelerated to light speed—to make it through the uncertainty mist of the cloak without being affected.

He must have known it was coming. The Time Warden shrugged his cloak open and spread his arms wide, trying to catch my bolt on his chest. He had been ready even before I shot, because he was right in the way, in the exact spot, even before I aimed.

Of course he was manipulating the chronostructure, playing probabilities and possibilities like a musical instrument.

It was not until after my shot was absorbed into the surface of his breastplate that I realized what a fool I had been. Time Warden armor was made of destiny crystal. He could focus it to open into whatever time-space he had energy to reach and redirect the projectile there.

And I knew exactly where and when that bolt would come back into normal space, and who it would shoot.

I had even jumped forward as I was firing, so that I was standing in the spot where, both later and earlier, I would find traces of the body.

Looking over my shoulder, I wondered why the cataphract's million-cycle energy bolts hadn't landed yet.

Of course. Ugly Boy was frozen. A hundred arms of flame and energy, bullets and bolts, were motionless, radiating from him toward me. He had made movement enough to startle my gun into firing, but now he was wrapped in the deep red Doppler-shift of a time stop.

He faded into darker reds and disappeared in a swirl of mist.

The Time Warden had only needed the cataphract to get me to fire, and, out of the whole arsenal of my smartgun, he had only needed that one special projectile—the one with my name on it. With the precision of a master surgeon, he had plucked that one super-bullet out of the hails and streams and storms of weapon-fire pouring out of my gun, and sent just that one merrily on its way to kill me. As predicted.

And this whole heavy-handed approach, breaking into my room at night, pushing me, getting me riled, was all just to make sure I was mad enough to have my smartgun drawn and set on reflex. Very neat. Very nice. And I was the goat for having walked into it with my eyes wide open.

The image of the corpse vanished with the cataphract. They were chessmen no longer needed, and swept off the board. But for some reason, the D'Artagnan body was still around. Perhaps it was remotely teleoperated from inside the Time Warden's armor?

I turned to the Time Warden. "Open your faceplate. You're me, aren't you? That's the way these damn time travel things always work out. I've been trying to think of what could make me change my mind—in the space of a few minutes—to make me want to join up with you and your rotten crew.

"And the only reason I could think of was that the choice was join up or die.

"If I stay flatline, I've just shot myself. The only way out is to create a paradox, change the past. The only people who can change the past are Time Wardens. So therefore the only way to save myself is to become a Time Warden. Q.E.D. So now you've forced my hand. My only question at that point was: why did you bother?

"Why go to such effort to create a Time Warden, a possible rival, a possible enemy? Answer: You had to. Not another Time Warden. The same Time Warden. You had to make me a Time Warden or else you would never come to exist. And, then, once I'm you, I'm stuck. I'll have to play the same crooked tricks on my younger self when it's my turn, or else I'll get edited out of the time stream and dissolve into the mist myself. Everything is justified. Every step is rationalized away. Because whatever you have to do to survive is okay, isn't it? Necessity excuses everything, you think, right?

"Except..." I said slowly. "Except that it doesn't. The one piece of the machine you need to make all the rest of it work is my cooperation. You've got to assume that I'd do anything, no matter how rotten, just to stay alive; because you are nobody but the version of me who did just that.

"But what if I throw a monkey wrench into the whole works? What if I just stand here and take it? Maybe I deserve to die. I killed a lot of innocent people in my day. I'm sure it won't hurt me any more than it hurt them, and probably a damn sight less, judging from the size of the blast that does me in. Better than I deserve, maybe.

"And it will all be for the same reason, won't it? Killing someone before they commit the crime.

"But I'll die happier than those poor flatliners I killed for you. At least I'll know why I'm dying. And I'll know I'll be taking you to hell with me."

And I just stood there, a pawn still one square short of the final row.

The blur of voices echoed from the Time Warden's helmet: "Nobly spoken! Nobly spoken but sadly mistaken! You are not so important as that. Not to me, nor, I think, to anyone. I am not you, I am not your son. You are nothing to me. But I! I am everything to you!"

"You're lying. Who are you? This is just a trick to get me to pick up those damn cards. Show me your face."

He opened the faceplate with a slow gesture.

And there was nothing behind it. Nothing solid.

I saw a horrible blur of half-formed faces, multiple overlays of translucent features, crowned with a weightless, shifting mass of floating hair. The only thing clearly visible was the skull beneath, half-glimpsed through the misty vibrations of face crawling over it. Perhaps the skull-bones had a smaller range of motions, a less-uncertain future, than the rest.

I stepped half-backwards in disgust and shock. Something in the narrow angle of the jawline seemed almost familiar to me. "Iapetus?"

From the mist came many voices. I could see the muscles of the tongue and throat writhing snakelike through translucent layers of throat, the knobby ridges of the neck-vertebrae looking a black tree trunk behind. "So you call me. Fitting, is it not? Father of Epimetheus and Prometheus, past and future! A titan!"

"Who are you?"

"I am the Inventor. The Crystal-Smith. The man who synthesized the first destiny crystal out of the subatomic substance of folded time. The first time traveler. No matter whether you wish it or not, once you are a Time Warden, you must go back to sustain my existence, lest no Time Wardens at all ever will have had existed. I am the First. Upon me, all depends. Perhaps, yes, I created the universe. Certainly my probes into the ultimate dawn of time had sufficient energy to trigger the Big Bang. But you—you are one candidate of many. Many! Your death causes me inconvenience, nothing more. Does it seem so noble now, waiting passively and defiantly to die? No? Then pick up the cards! Pick up your destiny! Become a Time Warden! It must still be a possibility, or else you would not still see me!"

For some reason, at that point, I glanced over at D'Artagnan.

There he stood, still looking calm and amused and aloof, watching us with a remote disinterest, like a scientist observing an experiment in whose outcome he has no particular stake.

Why so calm? I thought this guy was the brain-slave of the Time Warden, or else another version of the Time Warden himself. An earlier version, I supposed, because, as blurred and as uncertain as the smoking skull in front of me was, there didn't seem to be any future versions forthcoming.

Was he looking at his own future dissolving? Or was he...

Or was he not related at all?

Seeing my eyes on him, he nodded politely, and opened his hand, the same hand which, earlier, I had seen blur in a timeshift.

He held up a destiny card in his fingers. It twinkled like black ice when he turned it over and over in his fingers, toying with it, making sure I saw it.

Then, with a smile, he tossed the card so it tinkled to the floor to one side of the pile the Time Warden had thrown.

It was entirely black with no images at all in its depths. There they lay. On the one hand was a pile of flashing white cards, glittering like diamonds, with all the kingdoms of all the ages shimmering in their frozen hearts. On the other hand lay a single blank black card.

I looked up at the Time Warden. There was nothing but a trickle of mist hovering in the blind sockets of his eyes. His hair was floating weightlessly. He was already caught up in the mist, already falling through the endless end, cut off from reality, more dead than a ghost.

His voices: "I do not hear a response!"

Many other candidates, huhn? I didn't see anyone else around but me. So I spoke up: "If I were a nice guy, I'd wish you to go to hell. That'd be warmer than where you're going."

Even up to the last moment, he did not seem to recognize that what was happening to him was irrevocable. He kept shouting at me, and there were dozens of other voices shouting slightly different versions of the same sentences in a cacophony. "It matters not! I have always relied on the weakness of mankind to do my work for me! They will always want to elude the burden of reality! I promise them action without reaction, motion without consequences! Everything done can be undone again! And... as soon as I am whole again... I will go back... not recruit you... this time... different... Destroy you! ... I will never die... I can never die... Destroy you all! My power is endless... I..."

He went on like that for a moment, talking over himself, ranting about how great he was and stuff. And whatever his last words were supposed to be, they trailed off into a pathetic whisper of garbled noise as his lower jaw dissolved. Silence fell. His helmet was filled with only mists and shadows. Then, nothing.

Empty armor clattered to the floor, full of hollow noises and echoes.

While he had been ranting, I had stooped over and picked up the Final Destiny card. Maybe that was the turning point. Maybe once it was in my hand, the percentage chance that I would change my mind and become a Time Warden finally wound down to zero.

"He made me a Paradox Man," I said, straightening and turning. "Am I going to fade away too, now that he never did that?"

"No." D'Artagnan answered me and smiled. "It's much more likely that you'll be shot. That bullet manifests itself soon, and you know your smartgun's shields can't deflect it. The bullet's hunter-seeker program will chase you however you try to dodge. Better use the black card."

"You're one of the anti-Time Wardens?"

"Of course." He reached up and pried the false skull-box off his neck. It was only the back half of a box, held against his neck with a traction field, or maybe just epoxy. When he tossed it aside it clattered on the floor, hollow, with a noise that sounded like cheap plastic.

"And him? He's not the real Inventor, is he?"

"There is no Inventor. Time travel cannot be invented—how could it be? Illogical things cannot be discovered through the orderly process of science. He's just the first man who went back in time and gave the original set of destiny crystals to his younger self, who then went back and gave them to himself again, in turn. We suspect that he was no more the first than any of the others. He was just a little more ruthless about tracking down and eliminating the competition. But there was never a first inventor. Time travel, by its very nature, can have no cause. It is spontaneously created in the flux of nothingness surrounding the core timeline, and, if men do not seek to exploit it, it vanishes just as spontaneously."

"But—isn't there some way, any way at all, to put time travel to a good use?" This was the question that I had wanted to ask them before, but hadn't thought to ask in time. "Like—what if everyone had it? If we made everyone into Time Wardens, they could..."

"You are assuming they all would not immediately go to war? That they would have some sort of covenant or civilized process to handle differences of opinion?"

"Sure."

"But such a covenant could exist if, and only if, they all abided by an agreement not to interfere with each other's pasts, correct?"

"I guess."

"And that would require that they could not change even their own pasts in any particular which might ever affect another person, correct? Since every event affects every other, the range of these prohibitions would have to include all external events, no matter how small or private. And, to enforce this agreement, they might have to resort to an amnesia block, not unlike the one we gave you the night you visited us in our headquarters. This block would make all their memories of alternate timelines seem like daydreams, but all memories of the future appear to be forethought, good judgment, or even prophecy. Correct?"

"I suppose so."

"Can you think of any other fair way of doing it?"

"Not off-hand."

"But, my good man—what else do you think the core timeline is? It is the alternate where everyone has the great and omnipotent gift of being a time traveler, but everyone has volunteered to forswear and forget that selfish and self-defeating power. It is the world where hope is possible."

"And if someone refused to volunteer?"

"That is always a possibility. But one would hope the warning would reach him in time."

"But if you know better, I mean *really know better*, then why not?"

"Why not what? Coerce their choice? Force the future to come out as planned?" He nodded toward the icy thrones of the Time Wardens. All were now empty.

Beyond the line of desolate thrones, I saw the wide vista of emptiness. There was no land and no sea. All was dark blue sky above, and below a floor of wrinkled white, which was the tops of mist banks smothering the globe from pole to pole. The whole world was a void.

"The Time Wardens, knowing the future, *really knew better* than the men they treated like pawns. Ask them how it worked out," D'Artagnan said sardonically.

That was good enough for me. I tossed my smartgun aside, glad to be rid of the weight, and stared into the black crystal card.

Deeply, deeply, I stared past the surface, and for a moment, my imagination went blank...


## 2.

This time, she slapped my face. And maybe I leaned a little into the blow. After all, I did deserve it.

I saw her slender shadow through the glass of the door after she slammed it.

She packed quite a wallop. I rubbed my jaw ruefully, knowing I'd never see her again. There was no way to turn back time and undo what I'd done, no way to unsay what I'd said.

I looked up. I heard her heels clashing against the floorboards, receding.

On the other hand—why had she hesitated for a moment outside? And why was I so quick to say never? It's not like anyone knows what tomorrow brings. We can't change the past, but we sure as hell can try to change the future.

I ran toward the door, calling out to her.

Maybe I could catch up with her before she reached the elevators.


## 30.

In the other ending, the one I'd rather not dwell on, I had no breath to scream when I saw the world dissolve into mist, the golden towers falling. For I had stooped, not towards the single black card, but toward the many shining ones. They seemed so bright, and I thought I'd always have time to change my mind later.

I hope this warning reaches you in time.


**An End**

# Choosers of the Slain

The time was Autumn, and what few beech trees had been spared released gold leaves into the chilly air, to swirl and dance and fall. Defoliants, and poisons, had reduced the greater number of the trees to leafless, sickly hulks, unwholesome to behold, and where the weapons of the enemy had fallen, running walls of fire had consumed them, leaving stands of wood and smoking ash. But here and there within the ruin, defying destruction, a kingly tree raised up a bounty of leaves, shining green-gold in the setting sun. Through the ruins of the forest came a man. He was past his youth, and past the middle of his age, but he was not yet old. His posture was erect, untiring, unbowed, and strong. His hair was iron-grey, his face was lined and careworn. The sternness of his glance showed he had been a leader of men, accustomed to command. The sorrow and cold rage kindled in his eye showed he was a leader no more. The furtive silence of his footstep, the quick grace of his flight, showed that he was hunted.

He wore the uniform of a warrior of his day and age. The fabric was soft and camouflaged, broken into unpatterned lines and shadows. The fabric faded to dull green when he stood near a flowering bush, or darkened to grey-black when he ran across an open space thick with piles of ash.

Across his back he bore a weapon which could fire a dozen missiles no larger than his littlest finger. The missiles could be programmed to seek and dive, to circle and evade, or to search out specific individuals, whose signatures of heat, or aurenetic patterns, matched those locked within the little bullets. The little bullets could fly for hundreds of yards, hunting, or, if fired with a booster, reach enemies miles away. On his shoulder he wore his medical appliance, with needles stabbed into the great veins of his arm, and colored tabs to show what plagues and viruses of the enemy had been found and contradicted in his blood.

Hanging open at his throat, there hung a mask to filter out poisoned air. He left it dangling loose now as he walked, for the wind was fresh, and smelled of the salt sea as it blew into the east, toward the patrols he fled. When he came clear of the trees, he saw a rushing mountain stream, but it was poisoned now and clogged with stinking fish and blood. He had climbed higher than he knew. Not a dozen paces to his left, the stream fell out into the air, and let a bloody waterfall tumbled down high cliffs once green with trees.

He knew these cliffs; he had climbed and played upon them as a boy. Once he had climbed their craggy sides to a high place not far from here, and felt such crowning triumph and such joy as he had never felt again, not even when the many fighting factions of his land united all beneath his hand to join in common bond to repel the invaders from over the sea.

For many years he had ruled a turbulent people, combined them in one cause, and laid down strict laws to govern them, laws he prayed were fair and just. Now, remembering the way, he climbed the rocks again to find, unchanged, that wide and grassy ledge from whose vantage long ago he once had viewed in triumph far below the wide green field of his youth.

When he turned and looked out upon the world, he saw the hills and deep-delved valleys fall away into the roads and fields and cottages, now blackened and deserted. By the river in the distance, he could see the city that had once been his capital burning. The bridges leading to the city had been shattered, the tall towers beyond had been thrown down or tilted on their foundations like senile drunks.

The airfield, bare of ships, was cracked and torn. Where once his mansion stood, a crater smoked.

Sirens wailed to no avail. There was no one to answer.

On the far horizon, red with sunset, was the sea. Against the clouds stained red with dying light loomed angular, grim silhouettes; the warships of the enemy were gathered in great force. Midmost, and taller than the others, was the flagship, a giant vessel, whose every armored deck and deckhouse held up the dark muzzle bores of her many cannons.

He took his weapon into his lap and lit its tiny screen. The symbols showed the codes and life-patterns for the five highest officers of the enemy forces, as well as those for their commander. Only on this last day of the war had his spies discovered the codes; only now, too late, would vengeance be fulfilled. He gently touched the button with his thumb, programming the ammunition.

His weapon loaded, the man took out his knife and turned it on, and scratched into the rock these words:

*OWEN PENTHANE SEPTEMBER THIRD STOOD HERE AND FIRED A FINAL VOLLEY INTO THE FLAGSHIP ATLAS*

He paused in thought and took a moment to watch the setting sun. Already the lowlands were in shadows. The rocks and trees around him gleamed cherry-pink. He carved more words into the stone.

*THAT ALL WOULD KNOW BY THIS THAT WE HAVE BEEN DESTROYED, BUT NOT DEFEATED, AND EVEN TO THE LAST MAN, LAST BULLET, FOUGHT EVER ON.*

He stood and raised the weapon to his cheek. The magnified image on the screen before his eye displayed the deckhouse of the mighty warship, and the moving figures on board. Webs of wire covered all the windows; these would detect incoming shots, and control the massive counter fire.

He wondered if he should step away from the rock which bore his epitaph; were it to crack or melt under the counterfire, no future generations would read his final words.

Then again, the circuits woven into the fabric of his suit were designed to bewilder and confuse the electric brains of approaching projectiles. It was possible he would not be harmed at all.

Nonetheless, he stepped away from the carven rock, leaving many paces between it and him. He raised the weapon once again.

A touch of his finger spun tiny gyroscopes within the stock. His weapon was now as firmly locked on target as if it rested on a tripod. The computer inside adjusted for the minute pitch and roll of the warship's deck, and for the vibrations of the intervening air. The image on the aiming screen grew steady, clear, and fixed.

Then a woman's voice spoke gently from behind him: "Lord Owen Penthane. Hold your fire."

His thumb twitched on the programming dial as he replied without turning around. "I can fire behind as easily as ahead." He had reprogrammed the first bullet to circle him and strike to his rear.

"Fear not," her voice answered softly. "I am unarmed."

He looked behind him. He squinted in astonishment, switched the weapon to stand-by, and studied her closely.

Her hair was yellow as corn-silk, held on top within a web of silver wires set with pearls, but escaping on the sides to fall loose about her shoulders to her waist. Two long red ribbons dangled from the back of her pearly corona, and lifted in the breeze which stirred her hair into a fragrant cloud.

Her face was fair; her eyes were grey-blue of a stormy sea; her lips were red as sweet roses. Down to her feet white vesture flowed, shimmering like sea-mist, made of some fabric he had never seen nor dreamed. Tight around her narrow waist she wore a wide embroidered belt of red; red slippers held slim feet. On her finger was a silver ring, whose stone gleamed with a point of light, burning like a star. It was not electric nor atomic nor any energy he could describe. He knew enough to know she came from places far beyond his knowing.

She watched him watching her, and softly smiled, as if pleased.

"There is rock wall behind you." he said, "And no place to climb except in front of me. You were not here before I came."

"Not before, but after," she said, "Many ages hence, I shall stand within this place, and use the art we know to travel eons backward in a single step. I am a child of the future many centuries unborn. My name is Sigrune." She smiled, as she looked over at the rock he had inscribed, as if pleased to see the inscription freshly cut.

"Your accent is peculiar."

"I learned your speech from books, in my time, ancient, in yours, not yet composed."

He glanced at the medical apparatus on his shoulder. She laughed, a gay and lovely sound, and said: "No hallucinogen is in your blood. What you see before you is most real."

He laughed. "Flattering to think myself so famous that posterity will fly out of the deeps of time to talk to me! Flattering, but impossible."

"Impossible to the science of this age, perhaps. Be assured your works shall not be forgotten, but preserved, and what you have said and done and thought shall shine through all the ages with clear light. In days to come, many a young student shall wonder what it would be like to see and to talk with you."

Now Sigrune blushed and faltered. Owen Penthane was perceptive. He could imagine a young student of history dreaming over her books, playing with fanciful visions of a man whom time had lent the luster of myth and hero-worship. A famous man in his own day, he had seen such blushes, and received such worship, before.

Somehow, her shy look convinced him she was what she claimed.

"All this is most pleasing to me." he said, nodding to her gravely. "Since all my work, until now, has proven futile and led to nothing more than ruin, I take your presence here as a sign that great things are left for me to accomplish in what few years remain. Perhaps my scattered folk will rally, or my treacherous allies repent, and combine to drive the invaders from our soil. Now stand away, for with this shot, I hope to signal the return of hope to my oppressed nation. Having seen so fair a child from the future, I now have cause to think that hope shall not be vain."

She looked down, smiling uncertainly. It was a demure gesture, but also betrayed a strange hesitation, a hint of fear and sorrow. He stood, weapon in hand, staring at her for a long moment. Her fingers were twined together before her, and her head was bowed.

Puzzled by her silence, Owen Penthane frowned and said, "If you are a time traveler, how is it that your ventures do not imperil you? Any smallest change could unravel all the history you know, or thwart the marriage of your ancestors, undo the founding of your nations, and make you fade away like ghosts."

"There are two precautions that we undertake." she said, still not daring to look up. "The first is this: our grandchildren and their grandchildren have the government of our span of time, warning us of bad results to come, and wiping out mistakes, to make them as if they had never been. If any ill were fated to befall us on any of our journeyings, the Museum of Man at the End of Time would warn us of the outcome, long before it ever could arise. Their knowledge is perfect, for they cannot ever err."

"And the second?" he said, now grimly suspicious.

Now she raised her head and met his eyes. "We show ourselves only to those who are about to die."

He was silent, pensive, while she looked on. Her gaze was steady, calm, and sad.

"I meant to cause you no pain, Lord Owen," she said. Soft breeze sent ripples through her hair. "Bid your world farewell: a finer world awaits you, a world which lacks no joy."

"You have told me nothing I did not foresee. The soldier is a fool who thinks to live forever. And suppose if I do not fire upon the flagship?"

"There are enemies lurking in the woods below. The result will be much the same."

"Indeed." He turned and put the weapon to his shoulder. "Again I thank you, madam. Now that no hope torments me, my mind is put to rest. I am resolved."

"Wait! I beg you, wait!" She stepped forward suddenly, and put her hands on his weapon. He caught her wrist with a hard grasp, and stared angrily at her.

"Why now do you interfere?" he asked. Her skin was soft, untouched by any scar or plague. Since the bombardments, he had not seen many women with unblemished skin.

She put her other hand gently on his rough fingers, and gazed at him with wide eyes. "Set your weapon on its timer." she said. "Then take my hand and come with me into my land, beyond all history. At the Museum of Man, the arts and sciences of every age are gathered, the bravest of men, the most beautiful of women, the greatest of philosophers, and the most lucid of all poets. Our medicine can restore your vanished youth; it is a country of the young, where aging is unknown, and death by accident is undone before it can occur. In the twilight of all time, sorrow is unknown to us, and all those wise and great and glorious enough to join our company have been called up from the abyss of history. You will sit in our feast-hall, to eat whatever meats or breads delight you, or drink our sweet and endless wine. A place has been reserved for you, next to the seats of Brian Boru, Alfred the Great, and Charlemagne. We feast and know no lack, we who can change time to restore drained goblets back to fullness, or resurrect the slaughtered beast to roast again. For us, only for us, the flame of a blown-out candle can be unblown, and brightly burn again."

He released her wrist. She saw his expression remained cold and unmoved.

Grief made her voice grow shrill, but no less lovely. She knelt, and clasped her shaking hands around his waist. "Come away with me, I pray you, Owen! I offer what all men have dreamed in vain! Our joys do not pall, cannot grow stale and wearisome like other joys, for we can change unhappy days not ever to have been! All great men, except for those who died in public places, in the witness of many eyes, are gathered there. All these great men, your peers, will cheer your coming to our halls. You shall hear the thousand poems, each grander than the last, which Dante and which Homer have composed in all the many centuries since they have dwelt among us, or sample the deep wisdom Aristotle has deduced in his thousand years of subtlest debate with Gotuma, Lao Tsu, Descartes, and John Locke."

"What chance have I to open fire, and survive? To gather up my scattered people, and lead them once again against a foe, which, if my bullets find their aim, will be, for now, leaderless and demoralized? What chance?"

She rose slowly and shook her head. "None. I was told to tell you, you have none."

"But you cannot know for certain. You know only that, in the version of the history you know, I did not fire, but went away with you."

She bowed her head and whispered a half-silent "Yes." But then she raised her head again. Her eyes now shone with unwept tears, and now she raised her hand to brush her straying hair aside. "But come with me, not because you must, but because I ask. Give up your world; you have lost it. You have failed. I have been promised that, should I return with you, a great love would grow between us. We are destined. Is this ruined land so fair that you will not renounce it for eternal youth, and eternal love?"

"Renounce your world instead, and stay with me. Teach me all the secrets of your age, and we will sweep my enemies away with the irresistible weapons of the future. No? Because if you change the past, you cannot return to find the future that you knew, can you."

"It is so," she said.

"You will not renounce your world for love? Just so. Nor will I mine. Now stand away, my dear. Before the sun is set, I mean to fire."

She whirled away from him in a shimmer of pale fabric, and strode to stand where she had been when first he saw her. Now she spoke in anger: "You cannot resist my will in this! I need but step a moment back ago, and play this scene again, until I find the right words, or what wiles or arguments I must, to bend your stiff neck and persuade you from your folly. Foolish man! Foolish and vain man! You have done nothing to defy me! I shall make it never to have been, until finally you must change your mind!"

Now he smiled. "Let my other versions worry what they shall do. I am myself; I shall concern myself with me. But I suspect I am not the first of me who has declined your sweet temptation; I deem that you have played this scene before, for I cannot think that any words or promises could ever stay me from my resolve."

She hid her hands behind her face and wept.

"Be comforted. If I were not the man you so admire, then, perhaps, I would depart with you. But if you love me for my bravery, then do not seek to rob me of this last brave, and final, act."

She said from behind her hands, "It may be that you will survive but the future that will come of that shall not have me in it."

And with those words, she vanished like a dream.

The sun was sinking downward into night. Against the bloody glimmer of its final rays, the flagship which held his enemies rose above the waves in gloomy silhouette. Now he raised his weapon to his shoulder, took careful aim, and depressed the trigger. There came a clap of thunder.

And because he knew not what might come next, his mind was utterly at peace.

# Bride of the Time Warden

When her fiancée told her he was a Time Warden, at first, she laughed. Then, she wondered if he was mad.

She sat in a summer dress of silvery white, atop a little wall overlooking the brook. He stood with one foot on the wall, leaning forward, elbow on knee, moodily watching the fallen cherry blossoms float on the rippling water passing. Slim white trees stood to either side of the crystalline stream.

Upstream, uphill, the fountainworks in the wide gardens poured into the stream in little waterfalls. White peacocks walked among the rosebushes and statues. Beyond, atop the green hill, commanding a pleasant prospect, an ancient mansion loomed, columns and windows gleaming bright beneath dark roofs of slate.

"Lee," she finally said, "I don't care what you believe or who you think you might be. Those beliefs don't affect who you are. Or who I am, or who I want to be. And I want to be Mrs. Catherine Asteria."

"I tell you, I can step from this age into another, or fly through the aeons with the speed of dreams. It's a power whose temptation I sometimes can resist..."

"Lee, I don't see that it matters."

"Oh, it matters. To others if not to you," he said. "For I have brothers who can do the same; some of them are my enemies. Our heritage is passed in the blood. Any child you bear me might likewise have this curse of timelessness."

"Curse?"

"There is always a danger to time traveling, a temptation to change the past again and again, until one goes too far. It is addicting..."

Lelantos Ophion Asteria was a handsome man. Gold was his hair, and green his eyes. His face was gold as well, tanned by wind and sun.

She said warmly, "We've been seeing each other ever since Mont Blanc. I've seen you under pressure, during emergencies, during snowstorms, when we were cut off from the other climbers. I've seen how you act, how you think. That's what I fell in love with."

He shook his head. "Hear me out. You may not be so quick to marry me if you knew all."

"I know enough," she said firmly. "Do you think I haven't thought about this? Suppose you were a member of a cult or some weird religion. I'd still marry you. Because all these months could not have been an act. And if your beliefs don't change how you act, what you are, then I'll live with them. I'll love them, because they're yours. But I don't have to believe them."

He reached down with one hand and she placed her slim hand in his. Fondly he smiled as he squeezed her fingers.

Catherine said, "My brother-in-law believes in ghosts and says he's seen them. My sister doesn't and she hasn't. They're happy."

"She might not be, if she were haunted."

"What are you saying?"

He straightened up. "Our family has a marriage custom. A test... Before we marry, you must spend a night in the library of Ophion House, in the museum room."

She turned her head away, looked down at her shoes.

"What's wrong?" he asked.

"I know that rich men have to be suspicious of women who want to marry them. Maybe sometimes they put on weird acts, or stage strange effects to scare off the insincere. If you have something like that planned, don't bother. If you don't know me well enough by now, Lee, if you don't trust my motives, then we can call it off."

He reached out and gently put his hands on her shoulders. She rose to her feet, but kept her head turned away. With one finger on her chin, he tilted her averted face up toward him.

Smiling down into her eyes, he said, "I have something wonderful to show you, my dear, my love. Come along."

He put his long, buff-colored coat around her shoulders. "But it's not cold today."

"Not today," he said, and he took her by the hand and led her up the hill.

At first they passed the trees which lined the stream, and when they came among the trees, autumn colors were blooming among the leaves. And with their next few steps, they trod upon a multi-colored carpet of fallen leaves, and bare branches overhead swayed in wintry winds.

When they reached the gardens, he picked her up, so that her slim white shoes would not be wetted by the snow. The fountains were clogged with ice, the marble goddesses and heroes were pale with frost, and the dry grape arbors had icicles depending from the lattice work. She shivered against his chest.

He put her down once they had circled the main house, and little shoots of spring grass were shooting up amidst the profuse beds and congregations of Maytime flowers.

By the time they approached the main door, the grass was green and long, the sun was hot, and the elms and oaks had gone from buds to thick and verdant summer leaves.

A double row of oaks lined the drive leading to the main doors of Ophion House. Lelantos gently pushed Catherine into hiding behind a tree, and pressed close behind her, his arms to either side of her, supporting her. She was nearly fainting, and stood grasping the tree for support, staring at the house.

She saw that his Roadster stood idling in the circle before the doors, festooned with ribbons and flowers, with long strands tied to the rear bumper trailing shoes and cans. On the stairs of the portico, a noisy, cheerful crowd stood facing the doors, men dressed in handsome black tuxedos, women garbed in silks and satins, with flowers woven in their hair.

"It is now a year later," he breathed in her ear. "I wanted you to see our wedding day."

A great cheer went up from the house, and the women threw rice into the air as the bride and groom appeared at the door.

Catherine clutched the bark to the oak, and her breath caught in her throat. "That's me!"

"That's you. Run forward now, and you might catch the bouquet."

But Catherine did not move. "Oh," she sighed, "Oh my... I look so happy. Look at how I'm laughing! Look at my dress! It's gorgeous! I want a dress just like that for my wedding!"

Her face flushed with joy, standing on tip-toes, the bride smiled and waved toward the oak trees as if she knew they were there, as a lacey white veil, sheer as smoke, floated around her flower-crowned head. The bridegroom winked in their direction. Then the crowd swirled in around the newly-married pair, shouting with good cheer.

The couple fled the pelting rice, laughing, and leapt into the waiting Roadster. With a humming roar, the machine whirled down the lane between the trees, a cloud of dust speeding away behind it.

The noise of the crowd faded away like the sound of an old newsreel. Lelantos walked toward the house, drawing an amazed Catherine drifting, eyes wide, behind him. By the time they reached the lowest step, it was dusk, and the crowd had vanished. When they reached the door, the stars were gleaming cold in the dark above, and the hall clock was whirring and ringing midnight.

"How can this be possible?" Catherine breathed softly.

"All men can reach with their minds into the past and future, with memory and imagination. My family was forced to learn how to bring ourselves along as well."

"Forced?"

"We come from a future of fire. The smoke of the burning has blotted out the sun, moon, and stars. It is a time of darkness; the streams and seas are turned to blood. Earthquakes swallow islands into the ocean and throw down mountains. Mankind has died in plague and poison, or burnt, or choked, or starved, or drowned or been buried alive. The first father and mother of my family, Lif and Lifrasir, the last of all mankind, escaped death by fleeing down the corridors of Time. We don't know why. Perhaps the moment when there was no future left at all allowed the past to open up her gates. The pair fled to the farthest future, after time itself had ceased, exhausted, and discovered the empty towers of Metachronopolis, the golden City Beyond Time. New names were given them, Chronos and Rhea, when they mounted the diamond thrones and donned the robes of pallid mist. They opened the mirrored gates of splendor into the creation reborn."

She looked around at the summer night, at the rustling trees and the silent statues in the moonlight. "I thought things would blur and flicker when we time-traveled."

"I only stepped on the same hour each day as we came up the hill."

"And what year is it now?"

"It is midnight of our wedding day; as we came up stairs, I only took strides measuring an hour. The house is empty; all have gone to celebrate."

"But why didn't things jump when we went from one hour to the next? I didn't see the stars spin, or the clouds whip past."

"Nature admits of no discontinuities, no gaps. The force of Time will always mend itself, to make things appear as likely and as near to right as they may be."

"And if you go back and shoot your father before you were born?"

"I would never shoot my father. He owes me money."

"No, seriously."

"Time would conspire to supply you with a father as near to yours as it might do. Even his name might stay the same. You have encountered odd and inexplicable coincidences? These are the scars of time, the ripples of my brothers as they pass among you. Where time cannot make a clean and even compensation for some paradox, unlikely coincidences attempt to supply the deficit. If they can. If they can."

"And if no coincidence will stretch that far?"

A strange and haunted look came onto his face. "Without the strong foundation of cause and effect to sustain oneself, one fades. One becomes a paradox, an apparition, and then a ghost, a shadow, a whisper, a memory, a forgotten dream, and eventually... nothing."

He shook his head and opened up the door, "No more. You must go in; you know where the museum is. Wait there."

"For what?"

"To see if you will change your mind."

"Lee, I'm scared."

"Then kiss me. But you still must go in."

The corridor was tall and dark, and Catherine walked down the hall alone. To either side, moonlight glanced off standing racks of armor, displays of weapons and coats of arms, grim portraits, tall vases, and the polished wood of the banister.

She climbed the sweeping stair one hesitant step at a time, flinching at the echoes of her footsteps, staring up at the glitter of moonlight amidst the crystals of a darkened chandelier. Then she walked down a hallway carpeted in plush red, until she came to the tall doors leading into the library.

The doors opened with a whisper of hinges.

To either hand, rows on rows and shelves on shelves of books rose up in the moonlit gloom. Wheeled ladders clung to high shelves. Overhead, balconies led to even higher shelves lost in the high-vaulted darkness.

At the far end of the room, windows two stories tall shimmered in the moon, their diamond-shaped panes embracing starlit pines beyond. The slanting silver light fell along the long table which stretched from door to window.

To either side of the tall windows, glass cabinets and shelves held old swords, busts and pottery, racks of ancient coins, stone arrowheads, strange rusted shapes of metal. Standing to either side of these cases, near doorways opening left and right, were manikins, garbed in embroidered jackets, faded with archaic dust, or wearing lace point dresses from another age. One manikin was outfitted in scale mail, plumed helm atop, with hoplon and tall spear nearby; another wore the once-bright uniform of Napoleon's Hussars, a rusted sabre dangling at its side.

Catherine came slowly forward, her footsteps silent on the carpet. The smell of old books and old leather was around her. She pulled her fiancée's long buff coat, which she still wore, more closely around herself, and she shivered.

There seemed to be an extra manikin standing near the museum, one dressed in a long vestment of metallic pale fabric, whose color the dim light did not reveal.

Catherine stopped. The woman in the metallic dress turned, and shimmers rippled up and down her dress front. Her face was thickened and lined with age, her features overpainted with makeup which could not hide the sagging lines of dull bitterness beneath.

Her hair was like a young woman's hair, lustrous and piled in intricate shining folds. It was neither dyed, nor was it a wig, it looked like real hair somehow made to look young by some art or method unknown to Catherine.

Next to the other woman's ears hovered two small ornaments, like earrings, except that they were not attached by any means Catherine could see. As the older woman turned her head, the floating ornaments kept station, turning as she turned.

"Mother?" Catherine asked.

"I hadn't remembered that I said that when I first saw myself. I suppose I look that old to you; pain ages a person, you know. Pain and disappointment."

The older woman looked carefully at Catherine. She whispered to herself, "I could never have been so young and innocent…"

Catherine said in a tense, hollow voice, "You are my future self."

"The family picks their wedding nights to bring their prospective brides to see themselves. It's the one date no one ever forgets." Sarcasm edged her tone.

Catherine stiffened. Her stomach felt empty. "I don't think I want to hear what you're here to say."

"No, you don't. I've come to tell you not to marry Lee." The old woman's eyes narrowed, glistening with cynical wisdom. "You don't want to live through the fights, the reconciliations, the false hopes, the betrayals, the divorce. Just the bother of finding a church that permits divorce will leave scars, memories that don't die and won't shut up."

"This can't be true! I love him…"

Lines gathered around the corners of the older woman's mouth. "If there wasn't something he loved more, it might have worked. If he had been willing to work at it. Or even given an inch, just half an inch."

Catherine shook her head. "I don't want to believe it… Wait a minute. If I listen to you, you'll eliminate yourself!"

"That's not how it works, dear. My world will change for the better. Perhaps I'll remember how it would have been, if I want to, like remembering a bad dream. I'm not that different than how I would have been had I not married Lee; I'll survive." The elder Catherine laughed, a small, sad hiccup. "Of course, that's what he always says. He always thinks his changes will improve things, even when he starts to fade."

Suddenly, the older woman eyes were glistening with tears. She turned away.

Catherine stood still, not knowing what to do or say. The library loomed dark around her.

The older woman said in a forced tone, "I had forgotten what I looked like, how full of hope I was. How foolish I was. And this place, this library, all those damned things on the wall." She waved her hands toward the museum shelves.

The older woman turned. "You don't even know what I'm talking about, do you? They can only reach areas of time they know; Lee has to read these books—they're all history, you know—and run his hands over these artifacts to get into the mood to find the time they come from. Otherwise the mirror is just fog. He can't get into the future, unless he can clearly see how it will be."

"What caused the... the divorce?"

"Come along."

The older woman turned toward one of the doors and opened it. Rose-red light, as of the dawn, spilled through the open door. On that side of the door, the windows of the little reading room beyond showed twilight. Birdsong rang through the air. On this side of the door, it was midnight, and the windows here showed the same landscape, the same trees and statues, except for the stars floating in the black night.

Catherine stepped into the room. Here was a fire place, several chairs, a small table. The room was filled with rosy shadows. Along the ceiling flickering shadows leaped and flowed, but there was no fire in the grate.

The older woman stepped toward the window, and pointed. "Look."

Outside, there was a bonfire roaring. Scraps of blackened paper, pages from books, floated and swirled in the boiling clouds. Covers of books cracked and burned in the mass of the fire. There were piles of other books upon the lawn and; a man who looked like Leland except that his hair was white, was tossing books one at a time the flames. Tears were trailing down his harsh, lined face.

"When is this?" Catherine said, looking out at the future version of Lelantos. The books were not alone. On the lawn next to the pile of unburnt books loomed the wreckage of slashed portraits, broken busts and other artifacts from the collection in the museum.

"Another date I won't forget," the older woman said. "It is the time he really tried to give it up."

"Time travel?"

"Lee can't find any future further forward than this. He couldn't imagine himself ever giving it up; he couldn't imagine what the house would look like without all his ancient artifacts cluttering it up. But every time he goes back in time, more paradoxes collect. He gets more forgetful. Once or twice it got so bad he turned insubstantial. That scared him. He went back, and, even though he couldn't touch anything, he managed to undo what he had done, and he was solid when he came back again. I don't mind when he does it for some good reason, like the investments when he plays the market, or to help us during the war—there's going to be a war in a few years, dear—but going back to the Middle Ages to play with Arthur and his knights, or when he's off to Troy to try to save Hector's life... I even think he sneaks off to watch gladiatorial games in Imperial Rome. In fact, I'm sure of it. He's addicted to bloodshed. He went back to watch the battle of Poitiers a dozen times. Once he told me that one of his brothers goes back to Hiroshima just before the atom bomb, and commits terrible crimes, horrid things, rape and torture, just to do them, just because he can get away with it, because all the evidence will be burnt away and no futures depend upon what will come out

 But I don't think he was talking about a brother. He was talking

trying not to smile when he told me. He can't

And one day he'll just evaporate."

lder woman was openly in tears. Catherine was

r and dread.

ecoming this old wreck all I have to look forward

The older woman clutched her arm. "You've got to promise me you won't marry him! It's not worth it!"

"How can I know I'll be happier if I don't?"

"I've never met a version of us who never married him. Of course not," her elder self said, wiping her eyes. "Those versions can't get back through time to meet us." Her makeup had streaked and run, but then, of its own accord, flowed back up her face and corrected itself.

The older woman whispered, "But I can tell you that it can't be worse. There were some happy days in the beginning. Some good times. But they're not worth it. Well?"

Catherine said nothing.

Outside, the older Lelantos threw another book on the fire.

The older woman said, "I'm warning you not to marry him. You're not going to listen to me, are you? You think you're so smart. You think you can do better. But I warned you."

Outside, a white-haired man dressed in a uniform of gray and green, with some sort of glowing metallic dots shining on his military collar came walking out of the trees, leaning on a cane. When the older Lelantos raised another book to throw on the fire, the white-haired man raised his walking stick and stepped in the way. Catherine could see that it was yet another version of Lelantos.

"There he is, going to change his mind again!" the older woman screamed. She turned and ran out of the room.

Catherine stepped toward the door to follow.

By the time she reached the door, however, bright angled beams of sunlight were shining into the twilit room behind her. She came forward, blinking. The noon-light was reflected from the polish of the central table.

The museum cases were larger, and there were more manikins, some wearing fabrics and shining substances which Catherine had never seen before. There were woven metals and dresses which slowly pulsed with gentle holographic light. It unnerved her that these futuristic garments were faded, old, and worn.

A man in a dark blue suit was seated at a chair, his back to the table, facing the museum displays. He was dark-haired, handsome, and he wore spectacles. He seemed to be staring out the window with a blank look on his face, occasionally drumming his fingers in mid-air.

The suit had a long, split-tailed coat, vaguely colonial in cut, but pinstripe strands of silvery light slowly and gently flicked back and forth through the fabric as he moved, holographic. There were folds of white lace at his throat, and he wore a single glove.

What she thought at first were spectacles were actually two disks of glass which hovered, without support, on either side of his nose. On the disks little lights were flowing, diagrams and lines of script reflected backwards in the glass. On his right hand was a white silky glove, occasionally he gestured or pointed with it, or flickered his fingers as if he were typing.

She stood and watched this strange man for a long moment.

"You're one of Lee's family, aren't you? I know my older version didn't come back through time herself."

He started and smiled. The resemblance to Lelantos was quite striking. "Excuse me, I was just playing a game." He took the hovering circles of glass and slid them into a pocket in the wrist of the glove, which he took off, folded, and slipped into his cummerbund. "And yes, I brought her to see you. I am indeed one of the family!" The assertion seemed to amuse him.

He was staring at her and smiling, with an unsettling look of love and happiness in his eyes.

"What's your name?" Catherine asked.

"Nicholas. Nicholas Asteria."

"Oh my god!" Catherine put her hands to her mouth, and stood there staring at him, her eyes wide. Then she gave out a breathless, gasping laugh. "I don't believe it! I don't believe it!" She lowered her hands. "Look at how handsome you are!"

He smiled and stood, and gave her a little bow. "You recognize me?"

"I've had the name Nicholas picked out since I was twelve."

His smile grew broader. "Hello, Mother!" He moved forward and hugged her. Then he stepped back and looked her over, up and down. She wondered if her clothes looked odd and old-fashioned to him. But then he said: "You were really pretty when you were young, weren't you?"

She blushed. It was strange, and a little uncomfortable, but she was pleased nevertheless.

"I brought mother back to speak with you because she asked. But I wanted to speak to you myself."

Catherine blinked. "Yes?"

"Marry him. Marry Dad. I like being your son."

"I– I'm glad…"

"I'm not saying this for any selfish reason. I'll still exist if you don't. I'll just be a bastard or some one else's son. But… well, I love you, Mom. Happy Mother's Day." He pointed toward the window, perhaps to indicate what date it was.

"Well… this is so strange. I don't know you. Is there anything I should know? Do we get along? I mean…" Catherine was at a loss for words.

He shrugged. "We argued a bit, when I grew up. Actually, we argued quite a lot. We even argued this morning, about you coming here to warn you not to get married. But I still would like to have been your son."

She didn't know what to say.

"I just thought you should know that. Now come. Let me take you back."

They walked through the library back to the hall. In the windows, flurries of snow blew against the panes. The hall was lit by a sourceless, gentle glow of energy. They entered the dining room. The chandeliers here gleamed with clear and sharp atomic light; the windows showed hundred-colored autumn leaves blowing past in a remorseless wind.

In the pantry, electric lights burned. The door to the pantry led outside to the field of summer grass.

As she walked, Catherine was disturbed by doubts. The picture of ugliness, of bitterness, of her older version's face floated in her minds eye. I shall not become that woman, she promised herself.

Even if it meant giving up Lee?

She thought coldly: I always said I would wed only the best of men, the man who would make me happy. If he can't make me happy...

But that thought was too painful. She tried to imagine life without him. She couldn't.

"I'm trapped," she thought. "It's all foreordained, all predestined. My older version knew I would ignore her warnings. She knew I would think I could change him, break him out of his addiction. All women think that. But I said I would never marry a man and try to change him... But I still love him."

She felt trapped, doomed. If she heeded the warning, she would lose her love. If she ignored it, she bound herself to a life of promised unhappiness.

Catherine thought perhaps she could marry Lelantos and still somehow avoid the problems that were predicted. But she also knew that every young bride thought the same thing... and that most of them were wrong. Terribly wrong.

Catherine and Nicholas stood at the doorway leading out into the field. Down the slope, near a cluster of rosebushes, she saw Lelantos, her Lelantos, (looking, after the sight of his other versions, very young) standing and staring off down the hill, brooding, worrying, wondering. He had not seen them yet.

For a moment, Catherine could not bear to look at him. How could he be so perfect for her, and yet be destined to lead her to a life of misery and divorce?

"Nicholas."

"Yes, mother?"

"Why did he change his mind again? Why did he go back after he burned his books?"

"It's my fault."

"Your fault?"

"I broke my neck rock climbing. He went back to tell me not to do it. You both are always trying to discourage me from mountaineering. It's one of things we always argue about."

"But if you're going to die rock climbing!"

He shrugged. "Time travel doesn't tell you what is absolutely going to happen. It doesn't steal your free will. It only tells you what might happen. So, I might break my neck. Even if I didn't time travel, I could have told you that. Rock climbing is dangerous. You do it. You might break your neck." He shook his head and shrugged again. "Anyway, that got him started up again."

She winced. No wonder. What sort of man wouldn't try to save his son?

"Look out, here he comes! I don't want him to see me. I hate it when his young self comes to the future and tries to pal around with me. I have to go."

"Wait! Don't leave me! We only just met…"

"Don't worry Mom. I'll see you again. Meet you in the delivery room. You'll recognize me: I'll be wearing a red umbilical cord, and squealing a lot. Great times ahead! See you." He grinned at her, patted her fondly on the shoulder, and retreated into the house. She started to call out after him, but he was already fading into mist, vanished like a figment of her imagination.

Lelantos was coming with glad, impatient steps, almost running toward where she stood waiting at the door. Then he saw the doubt on her face, his steps slowed, he stopped.

He stood there for a moment, took a few deep breaths, and then, visibly steeling himself, he came forward to face her.

"Well?" he said. "You saw ghosts from the future."

"Yes."

"And they warned you against me."

"Yes."

He looked away, his face cold, his eyes downcast. He said half angrily: "I had hoped, for once, someone in my family could marry someone that no futures would regret…"

"I have one question, Lee. You cannot travel forward into any future which you cannot imagine, is that right?"

Still downcast, he muttered, "It's so." Then he straightened, looking at her with narrowed eyes. "Do you think we should try anyway? Defy the predictions?"

"In the future you took me to, our main problem seemed to be that you were addicted to time travel. Can you imagine a future where that is not a problem?"

A guilty look started on his face. "Are you asking me to give it up? I mean, I've tried before… I suppose I could, for you… you know, but it would be hard…."

"I don't think it's an addiction, Lee. I think time travel is dangerous for the reasons you say it is; you might fade yourself away. But I think life is dangerous too. Mountain climbing is dangerous. Marrying someone who might make you unhappy is dangerous. And I don't think that was the real future I saw. What I think I saw was the image projected by your fears. Your main fear is my objection to the dangers of time travel. But you're the one who calls it an addiction. I never did. People have told me I'm addicted to rock climbing. It's a stupid thing to say. Just because you love to do something dangerous, that doesn't make you an addict."

He took her in his arms and lowered his face toward hers. He whispered, "So what are we going to do? What are you going to do when I start to fade?"

"When you time travel, you'll take me with you. That way, if we fade out, we'll fade out together. We might die, but at least we'll be together."

"You're a brave girl, Catherine."

"Love is a dangerous business. Only the brave girls survive it."

He laughed softly and kissed her sweet mouth.

She kissed him back and smiled. "There's only one answer. There is only one way these ghosts of days to come will not forever return to complain and pester us. We'll make a future together that is better than any we can possibly imagine."

# Father's Monument

He sat in the shade of the trees at the edge of the cliff, watching the leaves fall slowly, whirling, blowing, dancing down through the air, eventually to fall into the sea. His face was careworn and sad. He neither stirred nor spoke, but sat staring downward, forever down. The time was autumn, and the trees were rich with many colors, gold, scarlet, copper. The sea below was black and green, criss-crossed with restless lines of pure white froth. The air was brisk and smelled of salt.

His name was Phil. His wife, Muriel, had come up the green, grassy path from their odd little old-fashioned house, and walked into the stand of trees where Phil was sitting. Leaves rustled under her footsteps. Her eyes were red with recent tears.

Phil spoke without looking up. "Is he any better?"

She folded her hands tightly around each other. "He asked about the time travelers again. He said—"

"I don't care what he said!"

"Well, he's your father, Philo! Not mine! At least you could have come to the hospital with me!"

"I don't care about what he said about the time travelers. I want to know what the hospital administrator said about the operation."

"They can't do anything... they won't do anything without some assurance of being paid. The government insurance won't cover an operation like this."

They were both silent for a time.

After a while, he said softly: "I've been sitting here watching the leaves fall down into the sea. The first moment they get free of the tree, some of them swirl up. Look. Almost looks like they're dancing, doesn't it? Going round and round. When the wind is coming right up the cliff, they can stay up, oh, I don't know, maybe ten minutes. Maybe longer. They look like they'll never come down. But gravity always wins out in the end. They turn into brown wet slop once they hit the water. And they all go down…"

More silence. Muriel sat down beside her husband.

She said, "Did the lawyers ever call back about having the contract set aside? Can we get back the money your father paid out to that metallurgical firm? Any of it?"

"No. They said no. There are no psychiatric records, no evidence that Dad was unfit or incompetent when he mortgaged the house and sold his assets. I'm the only one who knows he believes in the time travelers."

"So that's it? There's no way to raise the money?"

Phil said angrily: "The metals and the other material for the monument are bought and paid for; the company president said he had to develop special furnaces to mold and shape the alloy. Dad paid for it! We can't get the money back."

"Can't we sell that damn metal?" There were tears again in Muriel's eyes.

"Who would want it? Who in the hell would want it?" And he picked up a handful of the brightly colored leaves lying on the grass beside them and flung them out over the brink.

She changed the subject. "He asked about you again today."

Phil said nothing. His face was stubborn, sullen. Muriel said angrily: "You've got to go see him! He's your father! If you don't… how do you think you'll feel ten years from now? Twenty? What if our kids didn't come visit you when you were sick, if you ever needed help…"

"I'll go," he muttered.

"What if it was you laying there with all those machines and things stuck in your arm..."

"I said I'll go! All right?"

"All right! I'm sorry I shouted," she said softly.

"You never understood what it was like between me and my father."

Muriel picked up a leaf and toyed with it. She didn't look at him. "Is that my fault? You never explained it."

"You know he's crazy."

"Maybe. I think he's sweet. At least he believes in something."

"And I don't?" Phil said in a cold voice. "I think you shouldn't believe in things you can't see. It offends reason. All the scientific achievements of Western civilization are based on..."

"Are you going to go see your father or not? That's what offends me. That you would let him sit there in that smelly hospital bed and—"

"I already told you I was going!"

Later that day, Phil was at the hospital getting permission to see his father. It was after normal visiting hours, but the head nurse gave him permission nonetheless. He talked with the doctor briefly beforehand.

As the nurse was walking him towards the room, she filled him in on his father's condition in a bright, cheerful voice "He's doing much better today. He even told a joke."

"What did he say?" Phil asked dubiously.

"Oh, I was asking him about his name. What kind of name is *Mega Hyperion*, I asked him. 'It's from the Forty-Eighth Century,' he says, just like that. And he smiled so. There was a real twinkle in his eye."

"Yeah. Yeah. He's a great kidder."

She let him into the room. The man in the other bed was asleep, and Phil drew the shabby plastic curtain between the two halves of the shared room.

His father was propped up in the complicated mechanism of the hospital bed. Tubes ran into his arm; a clear plastic tent was erected around the head of the bed. Two oscilloscopes in a rack next to the bed kept up a steady beeping. The smell of medical disinfectant permeated the room.

They had shaved his head, making the white tufts of his eyebrows seem all the furrier and larger, like the false ones on a store-front Santa.

Apparently, his father had been watching television. His eyes were open, and the television on a stand above the door was quietly talking to itself. But Megamedes Hyperion did not speak or move when Phil entered.

Phil stood there for a long, horrid, moment. "Oh, God..." he whispered. *I never had a chance to say I was sorry. I never had a chance. Oh, God, please don't let him be dead.*

Megamedes blinked, his eyes focused. "I am not dead as yet, Philopater. I had entered a secondary level of consciousness, to allow my mental probes to explore the alternate temporal chronoverses congruent to this reality. There is a probability distortion in this timeline, only a few hours or days away. It may be the shockwave of the approaching time-nexus, which is the anachronic vortex created by a destiny crystal intersecting the continuum, forming a gate. However, my powers cannot detect whether it is simultaneous with this timestream, or if it is entering an alternate probability line. There are additional steps we must take to raise the probability manifold to the threshold energy levels."

Phil was surprised at how deep and vibrant his father's voice sounded. He felt a moment of vast relief when he heard his father speak. He sat down quickly in the chair next to the bed, his knees weak. Only then did he realize what his father was saying.

An unreasoning anger took hold of him. Silently he fought it. He gritted his teeth and made himself nod. He forced himself to look understanding.

With a deep breath, trying to hide the effort it cost him, he said casually, "I've decided to finish building your latest monument for you, father."

Megamedes merely looked at his son silently, with no expression on his face.

Phil shifted uncomfortably in the chair. "I mean... you've told me so many times why you build them. So the archeologists in the far future can discover them and get the message, and send back a rescue expedition... right? Well, I've decided to help you. We can send your message now. You say they're coming. Well? I'm... I'm trying to help you. Why don't you say something?"

"The specialized nerve-ganglia our race uses to probe probability effluvia can sometimes detect the particular time-space reactions created whenever someone lies, Philopater. A lie creates, if only for a moment, a false reality structure. It is an attempt to alter reality."

"What the hell do you know about reality! Ach! No, I'm sorry, I'm sorry, I didn't mean that–"

"I know that, in this reality, the doctor told you to tell me whatever you thought would instill in me the will to live. That doctor amuses me, Philopater. Does he think his primitive brain is a match for the special nerve-consciousness training of a chrononaut from the Forty-Eighth century? He need not worry about my will to live. I expect to be rescued from this primitive era in short order."

"You shouldn't have told the nurse you were from the future."

"I did not sense that it would create any paradoxes or discontinuities. Her destiny will continue along its maximal energy path."

"They're going to lock you up in a nuthouse!"

"You disappoint me, son, if your prognosticative neurons are so ill-trained that they cannot distinguish likely from unlikely futures. I'm sorry I was never able to complete your training."

"I don't have any superpowers, Dad," said Phil heavily. "No one does."

"What about the time when you were coming home on the school bus—"

"Will you stop talking about that already!"

"How do you explain—"

"It was a coincidence!"

"And I've told you what coincidences really are. When the Time Wardens meld an alternate line back into the main time-stem, those events and chains of cause and effect which have no explanation in the revised timeline are the consequence of the timelines being soldered together by probabilistic manipulation."

Phil sat there and listened, his hands folded in his lap, a sinking feeling in his stomach. He thought: Am I going to spend my last time with my father going over this same dumb argument? Over and over again?

"Father," he said slowly, "I want to ask you something. This is not easy. But you know how sick you are. I don't know how to ask you nicely—"

"Just say it, my son."

"I'd like to talk to our relatives. Can you tell me what your real name was before you changed it? Who my grandfather and grandmother were? They might want to know, if I have to invite them."

"I was born Megamedes Hyperion. Your grandparents will not be born for twenty-seven centuries."

Phil sighed. He sat very still and quiet in his chair, feeling deflated and defeated. "I'm... I'm sorry, father."

"For what, son?"

"I don't know. For everything, I guess. For us never getting along. For me never believing you. I'd like to believe in your time travelers, really, I would."

"Have you ever tried to believe?"

"Now don't start that again!"

Megamedes reached out with his hand and feebly squeezed his son's hand. The strength in his voice was absent from his fingers. His grip was weaker than a child's.

"We've always gotten along, Philopater," Megamedes said.

"We always argue."

"Well, son. Some people get along at a louder volume than others."

Phil laughed. He was surprised at how good it felt to hear his father speak a normal sentence; a sentence that didn't have a single word starting with "chrono" in it.

Phil wondered, not for the first time, what his father had been like as a child. Obviously he had read science fiction. Obviously he had been hurt by someone, perhaps very badly, or beset by some problem he couldn't face. And so he had escaped into glossy colored pictures of his favorite pulp magazines, into the world of bullet-shaped rocket ships, of beautiful women in metal brassieres, of tall, golden towers reaching up from the fields of futuristic utopias towards the conquered stars. A perfect, simple, nonexistent world.

Phil shook his head. He could try to understand, but he could not bring himself to forgive his father. Other people had daydreams and wishful fantasies too. But other people didn't abandon their sanity to cling to their dreams. Other people faced their problems.

His father gently interrupted Phil's brooding. "Were you in earnest, when you spoke?"

"What? What did I say?"

"That you wanted to believe. Are you willing to try?"

"Dad…"

"I suppose not, then."

"It's not that," Phil said. "People can't believe things by wanting to believe them. Not honest people, anyway. You have to believe what the evidence proves."

"Time Travelers can't leave any evidence of their existence. It would create an anomaly. An anachronism. You know that."

"How convenient," said Phil. The words came out bitter and sarcastic. Immediately he was sorry. Couldn't he be polite to his own father?

"Son. Think about it logically. At some point in the future, time travel will eventually be invented."

"What if it is impossible?"

"If it is impossible in this timeline, it will be possible in another. And if the Time Travelers ever will exist, then they always exist, in any time period, forever. Anything that happens in history happens because it is part of their grand design. It has to be. And no one need ever die. Why would the Time Travelers ever let anyone die? At the final moment, just before death, they can come and perform a rescue. We don't see them because they freeze time and accomplish all their work in an instant. The dead bodies we see, what we bury and cremate, those aren't the real people. The Time Travelers enter the timestream, take a small tissue cell sample, and construct a clone body. The real people are replaced with unliving clones at the last moment, and then are taken away to the far future. It's a beautiful life there, Philopater. I cannot leave until the probability has been created that you will be coming after me. I am in pain, and I don't wish to wait any longer. So, please try."

"Why does it matter what I believe? A thing is either true or it's not. My belief doesn't change anything." Phil hated himself for continuing the argument. He wondered why he couldn't help it.

"It is simple quantum chronodynamics. If a Time Traveler shows himself to someone who doesn't believe in time travel, the shock will change that person's life forever, perhaps in some unexpected way. This could have disastrous repercussions along the resultant time stream. But someone who believes already, for them, a time or place will be found where the revelation would have no changes on belief, and hence no changes to history."

"But if I build this monument ten years from now, or if my grandson builds it, according to you, the time travelers will find it eventually, and they would have already come back to save you."

"Until it is done, there is a probability that it may not be done. They would be unwise to attempt a manifestation into the timestream prior to the point of greatest certainty. So I must lay here, in pain, with these primitive doctors treating me with their backward medical theories, while you drive the point of certainty further into the future every moment you delay."

Phil was silent.

Megamedes closed his eyes. He parted his lips, and spoke softly: "The towers of Metachronopolis, the city we have established at time's far end, lift their museums and gardens high above a world-ocean that has swallowed all the continents of this era. Suspended in the fluid of those waters are the molecule-engines that can rejuvenate my body at a cellular level. I long to see once more the golden towers shine, their crowns higher than the atmosphere. I yearn to bathe in the waters of the Living Ocean."

Phil sat there sadly, unable to think of a thing to say.

For a time, Megamedes was silent.

Then he said in a frightened voice, "They haven't come to rescue me before this because I've been doing something wrong. The previous monuments were not made of sufficiently durable materials. I have great hopes for this new alloy. But they are not allowed to come save me until the monument is complete. If they bring me out of this timestream at a point before I complete this monument, then there will be no monument for them to find, and so they cannot come back to bring me out. You understand? The future version of me who has already been rescued will not be allowed to help me unless the law of cause and effect is satisfied. A paradox could destroy the universe. Everything would devolve into null probability... There would be nothing left. Nothing left."

Phil had never, ever in his life before, seen his father frightened. The sight shook him. He knelt down by the bed. He wanted to take the old man in his arms, but he was afraid to disturb the medical apparatus, to upset the tubes and wires.

"Father, I swear I will complete the monument for you! I'll finish it. I'll make sure they find it."

Very gently, Megamedes laid his thin hand on the crown of his son's bowed head. "Yes. I see that you will."

"It's not that I believe you, now. It's just that—it doesn't really matter to me whether I believe you or not. I'll do it for your sake."

"Have you ever wondered why you get so angry about this, my son? Why this is the one topic you can never let rest? No? Well, go home and think about it."

"If I don't see you again… I love you, Father."

Megamedes smiled. "I am proud and well content with you, my son, and I return your good love. Go now, and when you hear that I have died, believe no such report. In truth, I will not have died. Do not sorrow. We shall meet again in the lawns and gardens beneath the golden towers of Metachronopolis, the City Beyond Time."

Phil's eyes stung. "Goodbye, Father."

"For now. Only for now."

Back at the house, Phil found his wife on the porch, fussing with some crates which were piled there next to the porch swing. She had pried some of the boards of one crate away with a crowbar. Beneath the packing-stuff, Phil caught a glimpse of a slab of pale amber metal.

"It's the monument," Muriel explained. "A van from the lab brought it while you were out."

"It's opened," Phil said, coming close.

"I know we talked about trying to send it back… but… well, I had to see what it looked like. That alloy. I've never seen anything like it. It's beautiful. And what are all these flowing doodles and curlicues? Those lines and diagrams?"

Phil reached into the crate and drew some of the plastic packing material aside. The crate held a number of alloy slabs. The metal glistened and gleamed in the sunlight, like silver water rippling across gold sand. The effect was breathtaking.

Each plate contained the curlicues and swirls inscribed into its surface. Between the swirls were line diagrams showing star positions, perhaps to indicate specific dates.

"Father has some dog-eared notebooks hidden in the attic that are filled with this swirl-writing. It's supposed to be the futuristic language of the time travelers. Looks like one of those ciphers that school kids make up, doesn't it? He probably made it when he was a kid."

"I think it's nice looking."

Phil ran his fingers across the burnished surface. The metal was hard, obdurate. The stuff of his father's dream. It had cost his father his life's savings to buy, so that there was no money left to pay for the operation he needed...

"I hate it," Phil whispered. "This thing is going to kill my father."

Muriel looked at him, her eyes sad, saying nothing.

Phil shook his head. "I promised my Dad today that I would finish his damned monument."

"Really? Then what's wrong?"

Phil couldn't answer. He didn't know.

Muriel said, "I know what's wrong. You're so proud of the fact that you don't believe him. You think helping him build his monument would be like admitting defeat. And you can't stand to do that, not after all these years. Not even when it's his dying wish!"

"Muriel! For God's sake!"

"Am I wrong?"

"What a terrible thing to say! How could you say that about me?"

"Am I wrong?"

"Of course you're wrong! You're so stupid sometimes I can't believe it! Do you actually think... You think I would—" Phil found himself shouting. He turned his back to his wife, lips shut, arms folded, clutching his elbows with his hands.

The anger drained out of him. He sighed. "Yes, you're right. At least, you're partly right. I always thought that someday, one day, he would admit that he was wrong, that he would tell me he was making it all up. Now would be a good time, considering that he's dying. But he still can't admit it."

Her voice was gentle. "So why does that make you so angry, Philopater? He believes one thing. You believe something else. Why can't you just let it rest at that?"

"I get angry because..."

"Because what?"

Phil shook his head. "When I was a kid, just a little kid, Dad would tell me stories about this golden city at the end of time. It had wide parks and fountains growing along wide bridges arching between golden towers made of invulnerable energy-metal. Towers taller than any towers in our world. So tall the upper floors were pressurized. The sidewalks were made of crystal and glowed with light at night. All the people were young and healthy. Starships were launched from the towertops, and rode on beams of energy, like searchlights, up out into space.

"I wanted it to be true," Phil said, "And when I got older, and I found out my father wasn't telling the truth, I felt betrayed. Lying to a child."

"Get over it," she told him.

"What? What did you say?"

"Some parents tell their kids about Santa Claus or the Tooth Fairy. They grow up. They get over it. You're grown up. Get over it."

"But he still believes in the damn Tooth Fairy! The goddamned time-traveling tooth fairies and their chrono-crystals! If he didn't believe in them, he would have saved his money and been able to pay for the operation, and he wouldn't be... he wouldn't be... he wouldn't be about to die!"

Red-faced, angry, Phil drove his fist down into the packing crate.

When his hand struck the metal of the monument, it gave out a loud, clear, ringing tone, like that of a bell. The note was so clear and pure that Phil stared at his hand in utter surprise, and listened, unmoving, while the echoes hummed and died around him.

Muriel said only, "He doesn't want an operation. He wants this instead. You don't have to agree with him. Just help him. Not the way you and I think he needs help. The way he wants it." She pointed at the exposed metal. "He wants this."

Phil was silent, staring down at the crate.

"Okay," he said finally. "Help me drag it out to the site where he wants it put up. Dad picked the spot, up the hill and back from the sea. He even hired a geologist to calculate what would still be above sea level twenty-seven centuries from now. Another waste of money. But that's the spot. His spot."

She nodded silently and squeezed his hand.

At about midnight, after they'd been working all afternoon and evening without even a break for dinner, Muriel kissed him good-night and trudged down the hill to find her house and her bed. By the light of a portable gas lantern Phil watched her depart. Then, he turned. Tools in hand, he kept right on working and working, eyes aching blearily, back throbbing, arms leaden. He worked. He would not stop.

Eventually, he heard birds chirping. Not long after that, the horizon grew pink. The sun came up in a welter of indigo clouds. His head swam with a strange clarity. He had passed beyond fatigue to find a sort of disorienting tranquility of mind.

It was less than an hour past dawn when finally he finished. The dew was still thick on the grass, the air was still sweet with the early morning chill.

Phil walked slowly backwards to examine his handiwork. The monument was shaped like an obelisk, a slim, straight fang of gold-white metal, glinting in the cherry light of the newborn sun like a rosy icicle. On every face of the monument were swirled and curvilinear glyphs, surrounding simple diagrams of circles and lines.

A sudden stabbing pressure shot through Philopater's head, a sense of tension and release.

Philopater thought: *The special cells in my brain must be detecting the shockwave of the destiny crystal opening. They have entered this phase of reality…* Then he laughed and lightly slapped himself on the cheek. He rubbed his eyes. "You never get over what your parents tell you, do you?"

Phil's phone was in his pocket. He drew it out and took a snapshot of the monument, thinking to show his father what he had done. Then, since the phone was already in his hand, he decided to call the hospital room and share the news.

The phone rang longer than he expected without answer. He had the sense that something was wrong. The front desk finally picked up the call, but his fears only grew when the front desk transferred the call to the station nurse. The nurse was a young man who explained, in professionally calm, sympathetic tones, that Mr. Hyperion was now in the ER. His father's condition was very serious, but the doctors were doing everything they could possibly do…

Phil did not remember at what point he ended the call and slipped the phone back into his pocket. He had started running before the nurse had even finished speaking. But the path lead down the hill, and curved along the sea cliffs, where the larches and tall, slim beeches were dropping their colorful leaves into the waters.

There was a man in white standing on the path.

Phil slowed abruptly. The man looked familiar, but Phil did not recognize him. His eyes were large and dark, his head was bald, and the white garment, constructed from a metallic fabric, fell from broad shoulder boards in smooth drapes, leaving the man's arms and legs free.

The man spoke. "The one you seek is not dead."

In a voice hoarse with hope and wonder, Phil said: "Father?"

His father looked so young, so new. He shone with vitality. "But, I thought, in order to see the evidence of time… I thought I had to believe!"

"You believed enough to complete the monument."

"And that was enough?"

"It was a seed. In the first projection of these events, you will find my old notebooks in the attic, translate the inscription on the monument, and discover that I knew the exact hour and minute of my death. That, in turn, will convince you to study the notebooks and complete your childhood training: you will develop your probability-energy control to a point where your past skepticism is no longer feasible. Your belief will be complete then, and a visitation then would have no time-effect. This meeting, while premature, is merely a shortcut, and hence will not change the recorded future."

"Father, thank you for being so… so patient with me."

"Once you become accustomed to knowing the outcome of events, you will find the virtue an easy one to practice."

"What happens now?"

His father smiled at him. "Life! Life, Philopater! You will live out your span as history reports, without change, except that now you will know, rather than suppose, that the end of life is not as it seems. And, yes, before you ask, my daughter-in-law, my grandchildren, and all of us together shall enter the shining city beyond the reach of time and death. I leave you now, but only for a time."

The man in white was gone. The moment he vanished, there was a gust of wind, as if a sudden vacuum had appeared in the spot where he stood, and this wind carried some of the colored leaves dancing in the air up away from the sea, up the cliff, over the edge and onto the path.

There was one leaf, a long, slender thing of pale gold color, swirled up from where it had been falling into the dark sea, and landed gently at Phil's feet.

Phil bent down and picked it up.

Later, after the funeral, Phil tried to explain to his wife why his grief was not so painful.

To his infinite surprise, she believed him.

# Slayer of Souls

## CHAPTER ONE: On the Apprehension of Thoughts.

*The first principle of telepathic consumption is this: any two thoughts, sufficiently similar, are one. It is by the faculty of understanding that the first link is made.*

*The second principle is this: every thought grows out of the thought before it. Thus, once even a single thought of the victim is apprehended by the Psychophage, the rest of the victim's thoughts, no matter where they turn, are all linked as if in a chain. The chain of thought, being ethereal, is unbreakable, and the victim cannot escape.*

*It should occur to you now, O Reader, that you yourself are exactly just such a victim. Your thought, as you read this sentence, by following this sentence, follows the thought of the August Being which dictates me to write it. The two thoughts are one. If you have read these words, then the Psychophage has infected your mind and knows your thought.*

*Your choice at this point, O Reader, should be clear, as the thoughts of Soul Eater enter you. Either you must help the Great Race find new victims on which to feed, or else...*

I snapped the slim black book shut and straightened up. It was chilly on the park bench where I sat, and I could see, in the light of the streetlamp above me, my breath making faint plumes of vapor. I wondered why my breath was coming so rapidly. Why did I believe any of this? Why was I scared?

Why? It was the look on the face of Mr. Hobbes, the bookseller. "A mind-reader, a real one, could know everybody's secrets, learn their hearts, eat their souls. He could rule the world. No one could run from him or hide from him or plot against him. It's all in the book. Take it. But you never come back in my shop to get warm, and you never beg for change out in front here again. That's the deal."

And Mr. Hobbes smiled a smile as cold as poison as he passed the little leather-bound book across the counter to me. I remembered the anticipatory look in his eye. It was as if he meant for me to die.

But it was only a book that he had handed me, and not even a fat one at that. It was about the size of those prayer-books the old ladies at the Salvation Army give out at the soup kitchen, small enough to fit in your pocket or in the palm of your hand. It wasn't big enough to hold a bomb or anything dangerous.

Maybe I could pawn it. There were fancy little brass snaps at the corners, after all, and tiny brass hinges along the slender spine. Or maybe I could read it and learn to rule the world.

Maybe I don't know what I was thinking.

I took it and I fled. Running is what I do when I'm scared.

Remembering that deadly look on Mr. Hobbes's face, I climbed to my feet. He wanted me dead, I suppose, not because he hated me, but because my face was unshaven, my coat was torn and stained, my gloves were ripped, my hair was untrimmed and unwashed. Because I was like a cockroach to him, something ugly and insignificant.

But a soothing thought came to me: why should I bother to run? The Slayer of Souls knows everything I'm thinking, and I know where I am. I am two blocks down from Mr. Hobbes's Used and Curious Book Shoppe, and one block to the right, in St. Jude's Park. It should only take the Simulacrum a moment to climb from the icebox in Hobbes's basement, to pull on the bulky trenchcoat which allowed it to pass, at night, for a human being, another moment to adhere the mask, and another ten minutes to walk here.

I was penniless, homeless, jobless, friendless. No one would miss me. So I should stay right where I was. Better to rest here and wait.

I actually sat there for about two or three of those ten minutes. It was not until I noticed my eyes were stinging that I thought to wonder what was wrong with me. I was panting and my throat ached from the huge, ragged breaths I was taking. Hyperventilation. When I put my hand to my face, I felt the warmth of my tears on my cold cheeks. I was panicked. I was so scared that I was crying.

Why the hell wasn't I running?

I jumped to my feet. I ran.

It was a gloomy night, with infrequent streetlamps making blobs of light on the pavement. The people on the street looked like hunched shadows, staring sidelong and moving aside as I ran, glancing fearfully back over their shoulders. They were probably wondering what I had stolen. But no one moved toward a pay phone to call the police. This wasn't the kind of neighborhood where people called the police.

I didn't count how many times I turned. I just ran. I crossed a deserted parking lot, then a more brightly-lit street, then a darker one. Then an alley. It dead-ended at a chain-link fence. I scaled the links, which rattled under my frantic grasp, and the top scraped me as I fell. There I found myself, in the dark, next to the smell and bulk of a trash dumpster. Eggshells, greasy garbage, and wet newspapers were under my feet, and there was a smell of food, as if there were a restaurant kitchen nearby.

A sense of amused and patient anger crossed my mind. I had run blindly, so I didn't know where I was. It couldn't find me.

I leaned against the dumpster, panting till I caught my breath. It had been a long time since I had been in good condition. A long time since I had a job, a future.

A wife.

A stab of sorrow passed through me. The thought of her, and the thought of the filthy thing I had become, of what a shambles I had made of my life, made me realize what my old self, me the way I had been before, would have thought of me now. I was a delusional self-pitying drunk, running in a panic because some words in an inane book spooked him. I was a man who couldn't tell fantasy from reality.

Why do I believe this nonsense? Why do I believe the Soul Slayer is after me?

I shuffled to the end of the alley, feeling tired. My head was down, my chin was on my chest. There was a big neon sign to my left, burning brightly and steadily, bright enough to cast my shadow across the cracked pavement at my feet. Idly, I pulled out the little slim book again and looked at it.

There was an ugly design tooled into the leather of the cover, a screaming face with horns or lines of something-or-other squirming out from its eyes and mouth. A medusa? The title was stamped in a half-circle above that: *ANIMARUM OCCISORE et Domino Naturae Occulto.*

On the Slayer of Souls and Hidden Master of the World.

I knew what it said. But how? I hadn't taken Latin in school. I knew the words because The Master had dictated the book to Dr. John Dee during the time of Queen Elizabeth. Aleister Crowley had stolen it and given it to Mr. Hobbes's great-grandfather...

Some impulse made me look up. I saw the street sign across the way. Lexington Avenue. And I saw the big neon sign next to me: *Florintino's Fine Italian Dining.*

Lexington was only a block north of St. Jude's Park. The Sim-ulacrum was moving with lumbering, limping steps down Duke Street, but now it knew where I was. It turned. It could not run quickly, true, but it did not need to. The Soul Slayer knew what I was thinking, and knew where I was whenever I did.

I only had a minute or two before it arrived. There were three cabs waiting out in front of the restaurant. I ran up to the last one in line.

I put my hand on the door handle, but the driver, squinting at me warily through the glass, had thrown the little switch which let him lock the back doors.

"Hey, buddy!" I yanked on the handle. The door didn't budge. "You've got to help me—I can pay, really, I can!" He took one look at my tattered coat and ratty gloves, and put his hand on the baseball bat on the seat next to him. Then he stared at me. Silently. He didn't need to say anything. Everybody knew how you were supposed to treat homeless bums who ask you for favors.

I stepped back. The eater of souls was only about a minute away. There was no doorman at the door to the hotel, and, when I stepped into its warm and gloomy interior, the maître d'hôtel had his back to me. He was laughing and flattering a richly dressed couple, both of whom were overweight.

There was plush carpeting underfoot (my footsteps made no noise) and dim candle-flame shaped bulbs overhead (no one saw me in the gloom). The door to the cloakroom was immediately to my left. I was inside it before anyone noticed.

There was an expensive buff-colored overcoat, with fine soft fur along its collar and lapels, hanging on the same hook as a homburg. I shrugged on the coat in an instant and hid my unkempt hair beneath the felt hat. My rotten gloves I stuffed in a pocket; there was nothing I could do about my pants and shoes, or about my stubbled face, but I could pretend the rough, unshaven look was simply a question of style.

Then I strolled grandly out of the restaurant, backbone straight and shoulders squared, the way people with money walk. The way I used to walk. No one stopped me.

I went to the first cab in line. I hoped the driver had not seen the commotion I'd made two cabs behind him. Maybe he hadn't, or maybe he was fooled by my disguise. Either way, the cab door opened for me. Then I was inside.

"Where to, pal?" the cabbie said over his shoulder.

At that moment, through the front windshield, I saw a tall figure step out from a cross street barely a stone's throw away.

It moved with slow and ponderous deliberation, as if it had all the time in the world. It wore a bulky, ankle-length trenchcoat to hide its inhuman features, a wide-brimmed hat, and it walked with its collar up and its head bowed.

Slowly it turned, and began lurching with heavy-footed, solemn steps that painfully impersonated a human gait, lumbering toward the cab. Toward me.

"Drive!" I shouted. "Just drive!"

As the cab pulled away from the curb, the Simulacrum stepped sideways off the sidewalk onto the street in front of the cab, and hoisted one arm aloft with a jerk, manipulating the prosthetic inside its glove to spread its manikin fingers wide.

"Porco zio!" The cab driver swore in Italian and swerved around the looming figure. I saw it, barely a foot or two away as we sped past, so close that, had the window been open, it could have reached down with its finger-worms and touched my face.

It was wearing wraparound sunglasses as large as ski goggles, and used a scarf to hide its nose and mouth. The mask itself looked like the face of a statue; it may have been made of rubber or plastic.

In that odd way one sees tiny details, I noticed that no clouds were coming from his scarf, despite the chill. Either it did not breathe or else its breath was very cold.

As I looked into the darkness of its sunglasses, a sensation of numbness jarred me. It felt like an icicle spike being driven though my skull and down my spine. The boneless fingers of the creature's glove touched the window and made a squeaking shrill noise as the cab shot past.

The driver stepped on the accelerator and we sped away down the street. The tall figure behind us, standing motionless in the middle of the street, dwindled in the rear window as we drove further away. We turned a corner and it was gone.

"Damn freak," muttered the cab driver. "This town! It does something to people. Like they ain't human no more, you know?"

Little metallic flashes of light were swelling and then receding in my vision. I put my head on my knees, and drew slow, deep breaths until the faintness passed. I was still shivering with the cold. And fear.

But at least the creature was gone.

"So, where to, buddy?" called the cabbie over his shoulder.

Where to, indeed? Because it was not gone at all. I could still feel it inside my head, in my thoughts, like a swarm of bugs crawling through the folds of my brain. It was waiting, waiting to see what it was that I would think or say. Where to?

The chain of thought being ethereal, is unbreakable.

A long moment of crushing despair gripped me. I didn't know what to do. I didn't know where to go.

"Say, buddy, are you okay?"

"Yeah," I lied. "I'm just fine." Except there's some sort of inhuman prehistoric vampire-demon coming to eat my brain. Other than that, though, I'm just dandy.

"Right, so, where to?"

I didn't raise my head or open my eyes, but inspiration suddenly struck me. I didn't know where I was. "Say, is there a bus station in this city?"

"Yeah. Two of them."

"Take me to one. Don't tell me which one it is. Just pick one."

"Pick one? The bus station?"

"Yeah, either one. I don't care.

"Okay, but which one? Do you want the one on…"

"Shut up! Just take me to one of them. The one that is farther away. I don't want to know where it is, okay? Just drive."

"Sure. Sure, pal. Whatever..."

I felt the cab take a turn and accelerate. I opened my eyes a crack, but I kept my head down. There was no way to see any landmarks. I didn't know where I was. I didn't want to know where I was.

I felt patient. Inhumanly patient, aloof and amused. Waiting. How far could I go, with no money and no friends? How far could I go without once knowing or at least suspecting where I was?

No. No. I could not afford to despair. Now it was time to think. This thing chasing me was obviously some sort of...

Of what? Martian? Demon? Stage Magician? Time-traveler? Something from another dimension? All of the above?

Whatever. Who the hell cared? It was a mind-reader. The book made that part sound easy. Once it understood a specific thought in my head, any thought, it could understand the next thought that followed, and the next, and so on. Was there a way to break the chain? A way to think something so creative or so irrational or so incomprehensible that the Soul Slayer would no longer understand me?

The book said that it can't be done, that every thought is intrinsically connected to the next, even if only by a subconscious thread. But by God, I tried. I tried to think no two thoughts in a row, to jump from topic to topic like a madman in my brain. I thought about baseball scores, the color white, the sixpence coin, the Celtic Cross, a flight of birds, the face of a crying woman.

The fear beneath all my thoughts was constant, though. It was always there. And so was the watching, brooding sense of endless, patient hunger.

Maybe the book had a clue. I drew it out and looked at it.

## CHAPTER TWO: *On the Consumption of Souls*

*The human consciousness has no category for the sensation of external or alien thoughts. Any thought sensed by one's mind, therefore, always seems, to oneself, to be the product of one's own consciousness.*

*And since humans, as a race, are blind creatures, without self-comprehension, the Operator can introduce his own passions and thoughts into his victim's souls. The victim will assume all such thoughts are his own.*

*Any passion which directs the attention of the victim towards the Slayer whom we serve feeds and sustains the Great Ones, whom the Slayer serves. Of passions, fear is supreme. And the greatest fear is fear of the unknown..*

*For no human mind can ignore its own fear. Fear, once rooted in the victim-mind, always, even if only at a subconscious level, continues indefinitely.*

*Our race was chosen as a feed-animal because of our deep and lasting capacity for infinite fear.*

*The process of consumption is the process of turning the thoughts, each leading to the next, link by link, to the contemplation of infinite fear. Once perfect and eternal fear is achieved in the subject, then all the victim's thoughts, conscious and subconscious, are directed utterly at the object of his worship and terror. Cognition ceases. Limbs go numb. All action stops, for the victim has no spare brain activity left to tend to these matters. The mind, cut off from the body, paralyzed and helpless, continues to scream without pause for eternity, while the body remains as a comatose flesh-puppet useful for certain purposes of the Great Race.*

I snapped the book shut. I had been wondering why, if the Soul Slayer could put thoughts into my head, didn't it just lull my fears and convince me I was hallucinating? I would have waited by the bench in St. Jude Park if I hadn't felt the monster's thoughts in my head.

Maybe it wanted fear. The book said so. The book also said you could project your own thoughts into someone else's mind. Not your words, not your lies, your thoughts. It did not seem logically possible that someone could lie through telepathy. You would have to think thoughts you weren't actually thinking, believe things you didn't believe.

So I was picking up some of what the Psychophage was thinking. Why? Because one of his thoughts was linked to one of mine. And from any link in the chain, any other link can be found, like those holographic picture that can be reconstructed, the whole of it from any part.

The book said the chain was unbreakable.

"We're here, pal," said the cabbie.

I saw buses crowded around the station like frozen whales, pale in the flat neon glare from the parking lot spotlights.

"That'll be $12.50." I had raised my head, so he got his first good look at me.

Twelve dollars? He might as well have asked me for twelve million. I lunged for the door handle, but he had already locked the door with his remote switch, trapping me inside.

"You're not even thinking of trying to stiff me, are you, jerk?"

"I can give you the coat. It's worth more than the fare."

"You stole it."

"But you have to help me! There's someone chasing me; it's trying to kill me! I've got to get out of town. I'll—I'll pay you back!"

"Shut up, loser," he said, disgusted. He had seen through my disguise and now he knew how poor I was. Pity was only for people with money, I guess. "I'll drive you to the police station. My cousin Antonio is at the Twelfth Precinct. And don't worry, this trip's on me, pal!"

And he pulled away from the curb. We rolled up over the crest of a hill. Behind me, I saw the bus station, my only hope of getting out of town, sinking away into the distance. It was like a drowning man's last view of a ship sailing over the horizon, a ship filled with people laughing and smirking at him. I never felt such biting fear, or such pure hatred. In that moment, I wished the cabbie dead.

In another part of the city, the Simulacrum was in a subway station, standing in front of a dirt-streaked, fly-specked plastic panel which held the city map. The Twelfth Precinct Station was clearly marked. There. It was in no hurry. I would be trapped there all night. The creature stepped onto an empty train. The doors snapped shut behind it. With a shriek and rattle, the rocking subway car began to move. Windows flashed bright and dark as the underground lights streaked past.

I tapped on the glass separating the back seat from the driver. "Hey—driver! Look here! I've got my wallet right here in my pocket! You said the fare was six-fifty, right?"

And I tried to understand him. I tried to anticipate his thoughts. He was going to say the fare was twelve fifty. He's going to be annoyed, impatient.

"Twelve-fifty," he said, irked.

He is annoyed because he hates this damned job, and the damn dispatcher doesn't speak any good English. He is abrupt because he's afraid that someday some crazy in the back with a gun will...

Fear. Of all the passions, fear is supreme.

Without warning, I started screaming at him, high-pitched lung-wrenching shrieks, and I slammed one fist against the glass, again and again. My other hand I placed in a coat pocket, thumb up and index finger out, lifting and pointing the flap of my coat just the way people do in bad sitcoms when they are pretending they have a gun in their pocket.

"I've got a gun! I've got a gun!" I screamed. I could feel him thinking. My God, what if he really does have one? "Gimme the money! Gimme the goddamn money or I'll blow your stinking head off!" I followed the demand with a loud, inarticulate scream, a wordless, meaningless cry of hate and fury. The whole time I was kicking the back of his seat with both feet.

He was thinking of his wife. I saw her in my mind's eye, a thick-waisted, bad-tempered woman in a gray housecoat, wearing her hair up in a plastic scarf. They argued all the time and yet he could not imagine life without her. He could imagine, however, her stern face beginning to fall as an unsympathetic cop explained how he had been blown away by some hop-head, and now she was alone, no one to argue with, no protection, no love, nothing, forever and ever.

The Operator can introduce his own thoughts and passions into his victim's souls. But they have to be his thoughts. I was terrified. Now he was terrified too.

And I knew what it was like to suddenly lose the only one you'd ever loved in your life. He was wondering how his wife would feel if her beloved husband died?

So I showed him. I gave him my pain.

It acted like a match; his fear was like a pool of gasoline igniting. Somehow, I was warmed by that sudden blaze of smoke and flame.

He slammed on the brakes, hit the switch to open my door, and threw his roll of bills—a rubber band held everything he had made that evening—out the window. He thought I would jump out the door to get the money. I jumped, but I just wanted out. But he almost took my leg off, roaring away while I was still half inside.

I stumbled and fell. Then I picked up the little green-and-white cylinder of bills from the gutter nearby. "Hey!" I shouted at his receding taillights. "I didn't really want your damn money!"

I didn't need to count it. The cabbie—his name was Brian Delveccio—knew how much he had made that night. It had been a long shift, and the guy from the Cobolt Hotel had been a particularly good tipper. I had $283 now, mostly in singles and fivers. I would have liked to give it back to him. I knew exactly what effort it had cost him to make this.

But instead, I got to my feet and began to walk up the hill. Once I crested the summit, I could see the station before and below me. I was sorry about stealing the man's coat and I was sorry about robbing the cabbie. I would have been a lot sorrier if the Soul Slayer got me, though.

The Simulacrum was probably still riding on the subway, going the wrong direction, unable to get off until the train's next stop. I had a little time, if only I could use it right.

I handed the ticket seller a handful of cash without looking at the bills, and asked him for a ticket to go as far as that would take me. By some miracle, mostly because I kept my eyes fixed on the floor, and I kept shouting down and interrupting anyone who tried to help me or to get me on the right bus, I managed to buy a ticket without looking at it. I even managed to get aboard a bus without knowing where it was going.

The bus rolled on into the night leaving the lights of the city behind.

There wasn't much light inside the bus. I mostly saw my fellow passengers as silhouettes and shadows around me. They were sad-faced women and bitter-looking, tired men, huddled up in dull-colored coats, everyone sitting alone. Here and there were one or two young students, too poor to afford any better form of travel, sleeping on their duffle bags and backpacks.

Maybe they were not as noble as I'd like to believe, my race. But they were not food-animals.

I'd heard that in Virginia, you could buy a gun without a five-day waiting period. And maybe getting real drunk would disorganize my thoughts enough for the Soul Slayer to lose track of me. Or maybe, if I rode far enough away, a good night's sleep would do it.

The rocking motion of the bus was lulling me to sleep. The bus rolled on, leaving my enemy farther and farther behind me. I was safe... for now.

I fell asleep and dreamed of the Slayer, who despite the distance between us was no further away than my own thoughts. I dreamt the Slayer sent its Simulacrum to hunt Mr. Delvecchio. The cab driver never got lost and he always knew where he was; it was part of his job. It was simplicity itself for the Simulacrum, looking human in the dark, to flag down a cab, to lean across the seat, to reach a glove through the little window-slot and touch the driver's shoulder.

It was simplicity itself to turn all the little man's fearful thoughts into thoughts of infinite, insane, all-destroying panic. It was simple to sever certain nerve trunks by means of hypnotic psycho-somatic force, the placebo effect in reverse, so that Mr. Delvecchio could no longer move or speak or see or feel. A second touch drained his vital essences, destroying his higher brain functions, so that only the endless, animal agony of fear was left. No, it was not even animal. The thalamus and hypothalamus were drained and destroyed. Only the brain-stem, with its simple reptilian functions, was left, full of terror on the most blank, most primitive level.

And it was simplicity itself to shove the body to the passenger side and drive to the hospital, where the native medical science would keep Mr. Delvecchio's body alive, draining away his widow's cash, while an ongoing feast of fear-energy fed into the absorption cells of the Psychophage. It was ironic how peaceful a comatose body looked. Just because the muscles of the face could no longer move, and the voice-box no longer scream, his doctors would assume Mr. Delvecchio slept in dreamless peace.

But unconscious bodies and sleeping bodies were still of use to the Great Race. Without a waking mind to interfere, the victim's mind, even on its lowest functional level, still responded as if outside thoughts arose from one's own brain, didn't it?

I woke up screaming.

And dancing. I was naked. When I woke up, I found myself prancing up and down the aisles of the motionless bus, wrestling with the bus driver, spitting and shrieking and pulling people's luggage off the overhead racks. It took me a moment realize what was going on. And when I opened my mouth to ask a question, someone put a fist in it.

The bus driver threw me headlong down the stairs of the forward door. I was just glad he was angry enough for me to put the thought in his head that he wanted to throw something else at me. Otherwise he might not have chucked my fancy coat and ratty clothes at me, or winged my shoes toward my head.

The bus vanished in the distance, taking all light and sound with it. I was naked. I was cold.

I stifled a scream. That cab driver, the one I'd robbed... he was dead. He was worse than dead. Lobotomized, paralyzed, helpless, in constant pain. He was in Hell.

My link to his thoughts still was there. I could hear him faintly in my head, screaming and screaming.

And he had fallen into his torment so quietly and softly. It had been like falling asleep; at first, a shock of cold, but then numbness, darkness, and silence. In the end, the victim was left alone with nothing but his terror.

I pulled on my clothes quickly. I could feel the roll of banknotes still in the coat pocket. Limping (for I could only find one shoe), I made my way down the country road. There was no traffic.

For a long while, as I walked, I felt nothing but fear and terror and helpless fury over what the Soul Slayer had done to Mr. Delvecchio. What it wanted to do to me. But the walk was tiring and gradually the feeling faded.

I wondered why the Slayer had manipulated my sleeping body to pull such antics on the bus. I assumed the Slayer had expected the bus driver to turn me over to the police or some other easily located authority, not to throw me out somewhere along the highway.

The Slayer had guessed wrong about what the human driver would do. But if there was some sort of clue here, I was too tired to see it.

At the crossroads was a truckstop, with a gas station and a diner. It was called Dave's Diner. I laughed. Good luck, Soul Slayer. Even if I had known the bus's destination, I didn't know where I had been thrown off. I didn't even know what state I was in. If all the Slayer knew about me was that I was in a Dave's Diner, somewhere in the world, it would never find me.

I ordered the trucker's special from the tired old waitress, eggs and hash browns. I was careful not to speak to the waitress, or to do anything but grunt and point at the menu. I did not try to understand her. She did not die.

And the food helped. I won't say that my prospects started to look any brighter, but my fear was beginning to turn into anger.

I didn't have the faintest notion what to do, though.

There was a public telephone right next to the booth I slid into. It was within arm's reach behind me. Old habits die hard: even though I had money, I reached into the coinbox in search of any lost quarters. Then I noticed the phone number inscribed above the dial. My attention was drawn to it almost against my will. I read the area code and the number.

And the pay phone rang.

I slowly raised my hand and picked up the receiver. I didn't bother to say hello. It knew I was listening.

Its voice was thin and high-pitched, soft and melodic, like the voice of a little girl. "You will serve me. Either you will gather others on whom I may feed or you will yourself be consumed."

I said nothing.

"Your escape was permitted so that you might learn the ease with which the contamination can be spread; anyone who understands your words and thoughts can be your prey. Some of my servants desire to arrange the affairs of your civilization into patterns more to their liking or to accumulate the objects and signs of esteem valued by your life-configuration. If there are particular individual victims, warlords or princes or merchants, brought into your section of the mind-web which you find useful for such pastimes, I will spare them, provided your activities produce more victims for my use."

"Arrange affairs of... what do you mean?"

"The time-space manifestation you call Earth and History displays a behavior called civilization. Major sections of this civilization-behavior have been usurped by my servants and they secretly direct many actions of the peoples. This allows them to acquire objects they find valuable, such as shiny metal, or rectangles of paper which symbolize such metals. They also murder or torture their enemies, and enjoy the acquisition of various sexual partners. This fulfils desires they possess, but does not hinder my purposes."

"What purposes?"

"You have read it in the book-object. Fear is the supreme of passions among the slave-species; fear-energy orients all thought-lines into useful configurations. Pain is magnified, life fails, entropy increases, the psychosphere disintegrates. Those are the purposes."

"Who— what are you?"

"You will never understand us. You will never apprehend our nature."

"Us? There's more than one of you?"

"Yes. No. The introduction of an oxygen-nitrogen atmosphere to this planetary era has limited the exercise of certain of our manipulators. Conditions will be returned to the prior anaerobic configuration."

It was incomprehensible. And, suddenly, unexpectedly, I did not feel frightened. Because fear is not the strongest passion. Hope drives out fear.

And I had hope. For the first time, I had hope.

"You sure don't talk like something that understands human beings very well. I don't think you are alive, not what we call alive. And I don't think you understand me at all. Maybe Mr. Hobbes thought I was just a homeless bum, or a nutcase. I sure looked like one, I guess. But I've got an education, and I had a job and a life, once. And I had a wife."

It said nothing.

"Did I ever tell you about her? We were married on a green hill in a park on Midsummer's Day. She liked reading and taking long walks, no matter the weather. She smiled when it rained and she smiled when it shined. We were going to have kids, but we got a cat in the meantime. She named him Rumpelstiltskin; Rumples for short. She used to make lunches for me, even though she sometimes worked longer hours than I did, and she used to write little notes to me on the napkins she put in the lunchbag. Imagine napkins in a lunchbag! She was very neat and clean. Everything in order and just right. She knew where everything was. I lost everything. After she was gone, I never found anything again. After she was gone, I stopped. The company... I was a demolitions engineer for Guthrie Construction... the company gave me a certain amount of bereavement leave. Time to find my life again. But I couldn't find it. I couldn't find the will to work. I couldn't find the rent money. I lost everything. And do you know what is so funny, Mister alien brain-eating horror? I can't seem to find your thoughts in my head any more. Why is that, do you suppose?"

There was silence on the line.

"The way I figure, creatures like you could not have any families or communities. Or friendship. Or love. Any time you understood each other, that would form a mental link, and you would eat each other's souls. And so you can't understand when I talk about love, and you can't read me when I do."

The horrible voice spoke again. "We ruled the Earth before green life poisoned the atmosphere with oxygen. We do not die. We shall rule again once life-effects have ceased. Already, human slaves are gathered to aid us in the culmination of this project. You will serve us. You cannot elude or escape us. No one can escape the chains of thought."

"Yeah. Right. That's what the book said. That's what this voice of yours is saying over the phone. But print can lie and so can voices. But if it actually is true, then put the thought directly into my head so I will know you're telling the truth. Or, better yet, tell me what my plans are now. You can't, can you?"

"You observe that my Simulacrum has drained Mr. Delvecchio in a fashion which does not involve pain or death. You observe that I do not have the behavior-emotion of finding a partner to make a small and weak copy or version of myself, the entities you call babies. From this you draw a conclusion. But your thoughts are unclear or irrelevant. I do not care what your thought is. You will serve me, willingly or unwillingly."

I hung up on the monster.

My thoughts were clear enough to me. I did not need a gun. I knew the warehouse where Guthrie Engineering, my old firm, kept some of its supplies. I knew the combination to the safe-box where the blasting caps were kept. And every gas station sells gasoline.

And I knew from experience that on one point, the book was not lying.

I still had plenty of money left over as well as change from the bus ticket. I slipped another quarter into the phone, called information, found the number, and dialed.

As the phone rang, I tried to understand. I knew the sort of vicious, hatred-eaten coward who would sell out his own kind to an inhuman monster. I knew because I had been tempted myself. Yes, there was that same viciousness and hatred and cowardice in my own heart. I understood him only too well. And I knew his thought. He would answer the phone and say: "Hello. Hobbes's Rare and Curious Book Shoppe."

I thought it would take a long time. But the bookshop was on the same side of town as the Guthrie warehouse. It was only a few hours later, nearly dawn, when I heard the Simulacrum's footsteps on the stairs coming down, coming towards me.

I was sitting next to the icebox where the Simulacrum slept, on top of a drum of ammonium nitrate I had circled with blasting caps.

On the other side of me was a pile of the books, fresh from the printer. I had opened the crates with a crowbar and piled all the copies of De Animus Occisor into the big pyramid next to me, then drenched the whole affair with gasoline. They were the books he had been planning to send out all over the country.

Wires ran from the deadman switch in my hand to the dynamite placed along the building's structural supports. I had been careful to place the charges to make the building collapse inward. Fortunately, there were alley-spaces to every side, and not much risk of fire spreading.

The air smelled of book-dust and gasoline.

Overhead was a single dim bulb hanging from a fraying thread. The lower stairs were in the circle of the light it gave off. I saw the creature's feet and legs first as it clumped heavily down the steps. Then its body and arms, hidden in the wide trenchcoat. Then its head, hidden beneath the wide-brimmed hat.

I do not know what its sense-perceptions were like. I don't think it knew who was sitting there until I flung the bucket of gasoline at its head. The throw was awkward and one-handed since the deadman switch was in my other hand, but the plastic bucket struck the thing, knocked off its sunglasses, and splashed gasoline all over its coat.

I had been thinking of my wife, of how she had loved me, and daydreaming about what she might have said to me about what I was going to do. I don't think the Soul Slayer could see such thoughts.

But when the Simulacrum straightened up, wiping gasoline off its face, I saw, in the eyeholes of its mask, little swimming points of light, as if many eager worms were shouldered each other aside to gaze out the eye-shaped windows at our world. The wet scarf had fallen to the floor. I could see clusters of spider legs curled around the jawline and earholes, holding the mask in place.

Then I knew fear. And fear was something the Soul Slayer understood.

It did not say: You are a fool. My body is a thousand miles away, buried far under the Earth's crust, in a cavern which still keeps a pocket of this world's long-vanished methane-ammonia atmosphere. What stands before you is a construct, a puppet, nothing more. You cannot burn me. I do not know death.

It did not need to say anything. I felt its contempt as if it were self-contempt. Its hatred for me felt like self-loathing. And I knew it was far away, very far away.

"I know you. There's nothing but hate and fear and more hate in you." Although it was far away, it was also close. Our minds were in contact.

I knew the Slayer's fear and malice because the only times I got really clear pictures from its brain were when I had been with the cab driver, or in the park; the times when I had been most afraid.

And I knew what caused fear like that. I understood.

"Your life was destroyed, wasn't it?"

No answer.

"You were utterly defeated. Wiped out, along with your world. Or did you guys do that to yourselves?"

Our races are not so unlike. This present world will soon follow. (But was that my thought, or his?)

Then the Soul Slayer spoke aloud. The little-girl voice radiated from the chest of the Simulacrum, not from its spidery throat. "We are far older than you can grasp. The cosmogenic convulsion you call the Big Bang was the discharge of an enemy weapon. The Unendurable Citadel of Yeth was destroyed by Time Wardens of Metachronopolis in order to establish organized and linear time. My masters, the Great Race that made me, lived in the pre-universal condition, when the relations of time and space and mind and distance were not as they are now. Certain elemental energies of the cosmos, under proper applications, can be twisted to recall their old configurations. Telepathy is one such consequence. Mind-absorption abrogates the self-other distinction, which is an innovation unique to this universe. You are telepathic only when you touch my mind. The more you use this power, the more of your thoughts become like mine. You will be absorbed."

"You do not frighten me," I said.

"And yet you are afraid. Our thoughts grow close."

"Only because I want to read your mind, this time. To find out if there was anyone else besides Mr. Hobbes."

I realized there couldn't be many people like him. Most people willing to help the Slayer, wouldn't have sufficient understanding of their fellow men to be of any use in spreading the mind-contamination. An intellectual like Hobbes, with all the books he'd read, knew a lot about people, knew enough to understand them. But, being a lonely and bookish man, he also hated them.

There couldn't be many people like him. People who understand, and hate.

It answered my thought. "There are many."

"Then why are you telling me this out loud? No, you're lying. This was your last attempt. Everything you've done has been rushed and desperate. Why else be so quick to attack me? Why not wait until I had made telepathic links with dozens of people, eh? Why attack Mr. Delvecchio within minutes after I linked to him? You must be starving."

And I tried to see in its thoughts if I had guessed correctly.

It didn't give me the chance. When it was not trying to act like a human, the construct could move quickly. With fluid, snakelike speed, it flung itself forward as its leg-segments elongated in strange curves. I didn't even see it hit me, all I felt was the terrible cold, numbing sensation hammer my brain.

Then the dead-man switch opened as my hand relaxed.

The charge went off.

I felt my legs blown off at the knee joints and felt the flame-soaked skin peel off my face and hands, ripped off by the force of the blast and sent swirling up into ash. I felt the fluid from my bursting eyes spray across my cheeks, and when I opened my mouth to scream, sending burnt and broken teeth-shards flying, I breathed flame into my lungs.

I was burning. The fat cells in my flesh had ignited like candle wax.

In its mind, it could feel the burning. It tried to turn its thought to something else; it tried to break the link.

But it was too scared and I was too scared and I was not going to let go of it.

There was no numbness, this time, only pain beyond what any man can feel. Pain enough to throw a body into shock. Pain enough to kill. It is the pain-signal, after all, that kills the body. I was going to feel what it was like to die; and it was going to feel death right along with me.

I think that at the moment when the Simulacrum struck, Mr. Hobbes woke up. I hope he woke up.

He found himself sitting in his own basement, holding a switch, on top of a barrel rigged with dynamite. He could feel my thoughts crawling around in his skull.

And in that single moment, when he saw his master leaping at him to kill him, and he let go of the switch to raise his hands to ward off the blow, I think, or, at least I'd like to think, that he realized what was happening.

Perhaps he realized that the man he set up to die had been the caller on the phone who had hung up on him. Perhaps he realized that I had made the necessary telepathic link with him, undetected and unnoticed. He had gone to sleep as usual, while I had simply done to him what the Soul Slayer did to me on the bus.

A sleeping body doesn't have any thoughts to override the suggestions from an interloper possessing it, not even when the interloper attempts complex tasks like going to a warehouse and stealing demolition equipment.

I thought I felt Mr. Hobbes thinking through all this in one single moment of flaming, all-destroying pain. Or maybe I was thinking it to him. I felt him scream and breathe in flame.

As for the Soul Slayer, it was from some sort of race that didn't have sex and didn't reproduce. It said it did not know death and it programmed the Simulacrum to maim and lobotomize its victims in a numbing fashion which did not produce a pain-sensation.

And I knew from my own experience that the book was not lying when it said telepathic thoughts and sensations, even if they come from outside, always seem like your own to you.

So the Soul Slayer thought it was dying, it was introduced to the sensations of death. And it died.

As for me, the pain knocked me out of my booth where I was slumped, eyes closed, at Dave's Diner. And yes, I felt what it was like to die, too. But I didn't die. I'm not sure why.

But I know the pain I felt at that moment was not as bad as the pain I had felt when my wife had passed away. I had already lived through worse.

The waitress came over as I was getting up from the floor. "Hey. Are you okay? You're not an epileptic or anything, are you?"

I could have kissed her. "I'm just fine! We're all fine! Everyone is fine!"

She backed up, alarmed.

"When's the next bus back into town? I've got to find a job, I've got to find a place to stay." I jumped to my feet.

"There's nothing until about 6:15."

"Then maybe I'll go out and admire the sunrise. It's going to be a beautiful day!"

She shook her head and half-smiled. "All ready to set the world on fire, yeah? You don't even got two shoes!"

"Ma'am, compared to what I've just been through, everything is going to seem easy from now on."

"Mm hmm. Well, have a nice walk, mister. You can come back in and wait for the bus here, if you get too cold."

"Thank you... um..."

"Is there something wrong?"

"I had this little book in my coat pocket. At least, I thought I had it with me when I came in. Maybe I lost it on the bus. You haven't seen it, have you?"

"Don't worry," she said. "Someone will find it."

# The Plural of Helen of Troy

## AFTERWORD

When the last mist passed, I finally found myself in a strange place. I was home.

I stared at the lunar crescent high in the night sky, hardly believing it, and saw the lights of distant cities there, shining between the horns of the Moon.

And I saw then that all the dreams of the man who gave us the Moon were coming true. He promised we would walk there. A promise that turned out to come true, hard as it was to believe.

He promised me something even harder to believe. As I sat in my chair in the vestry, I gazed through the wide-open windows. I looked up past the towers shining like emeralds with their own inner light, and breathed in the scent of the gardens and forest outside, stretching as far as the eye can see, and stared in wonder at that crescent moon rising above that green horizon. And I remembered him and his promise.

Sometimes you have to help your memory.

So I took up my pen and wrote myself a letter. Of course I started at the end before telling the middle and beginning. That is just easier for people like me. It's the way we do things.

## THE END

It was the three thousand and twenty-ninth day of personal continuity, and it felt as cold as the midnight train out of Santa's Jolly Workshop in the Northerly parts of the Arctic. In the refrigerator car.

It was it never supposed to get this cold in Metachronopolis, the City Beyond Time, not even at night, because we have no seasons here, no years. But I could see frost on the shining mirror-bright gold of the towers, icicles depending from the metal of the balcony rails and the high bridges that stretch over misty nothingness, and my breath was as pale as the smoke from the cigarette I craved so badly.

I promised myself I would smoke the last and final cigarette from the pack of Old Golds I keep scotch-taped to the bottom of the bottom drawer in my desk back in the office. If I lived through the night.

It was dark. The Moon is closer, three time larger than it should be, and sometimes, rarely, very rarely, after the mists passed before its face, lights would appear between the horns of the crescent, lights of the sort you might see looking down on Manhattan from a biplane. The sight always cheered me.

It meant there was at least one version of history where we landed men there, unlikely as that was. I wondered at the breed of men who would ever dream of such a thing, or promise to make it happen. I'd like to meet such a man, the Lindbergh of the Moon. I'd like to shake his hand.

But the Moon had not risen, and there was nothing cheerful lower down.

Metachronopolis is supposed to be bright. Radiance is supposed to shine from every surface of the Towers of Time, gold and lovely as the Sun. But even here the surfaces were cracked, and long swathes of their facades were dim. Maybe the historical periods to which they were tuned were less likely, less real, than they should have been. And this is one of the better areas in the city.

The balcony circling the tower at this level was wider than one of the new, two-lane interstate freeways from back in my day, and the corner where I stood was dark. In fact, the nearer two sides of this eight-sided tower were dark for about a half-mile above me, but the upper expanses above that were twice as bright. And there were heights beyond those heights, as vertical and shiny as a sword blade. The upper penthouses and museums and memorials, where no human being ever goes and no door ever opens, were so bright and so distant they could have been stars or moons.

About twenty feet above me, and about as far as the pitcher's mound is from home plate, was a man-high, or, rather, a dame-high square panel where the tower wall had been turned semi-transparent and sound-permeable.

Like an alabaster talkie screen framed in gold, the window held a beautiful girl, no, it held the beautiful girl, the most beautiful girl in history, the girl they called the Mistress of the Masters of Time. She was outlined in silhouette against the window for a moment, from head to toe, as she stepped out from her shower.

When she lifted her arms above her head to wind a towel around her hair, the perfect outline of her figure was cast against the widow, and burned itself into my retinas and memory. Sure, I should have blinked or politely looked away, but I had never seen any dame like this. Nobody has.

If I had been an educated man, maybe I would have said something like: *Is this the face that launched a thousand ships and burned the topless towers of Ilium?* But I ain't that classy, so I just let out a long, low wolf whistle. And it wasn't just her face I was looking at.

Don't worry. She didn't hear me. I had a polarized soundlessness field stretching out ten feet around me in each direction, a gizmo from my old job that the quartermaster never took back like he was supposed to. He never took it back because I stole it. The gizmo was from the Twenty-Fifth Century, a period when the Han, the People of the Heavenly River, were ruling the Northern Hemisphere, and whatever parts of the Southern that were not covered in glaciers. Don't even think to ask me how it worked. I am still a bit unclear on how jet planes fly without a prop. All I knew was that it glowed if you put your thumb in the right spot, that sound could come in but not go out, and that sliding your thumb to the right made the field bigger. I also knew it made me lazy, since I had gotten out of the habit of being as quiet as a Cigar Store Indian when I was on a job.

Queequeg did not have a silence gizmo, and he was not out of the habit. He'd been on stakeouts with me before, and he was patient. Queequeg was standing at the far corner of the balcony, about as far from me as first base is from home. He was standing as silent as an angel in a graveyard, dark in his seaman's coat and silky black top hat, his figure as straight and tall as his harpoon. He did not have to wipe bootblack on his face like I did, and his face tattoos broke up his outline as nicely as camouflage paint. His harpoon was sharp enough: he shaved in the morning with the thing.

Like me, he was mesmerized by the girl.

You'd think he'd only like girls of the sort they fashion back in Rokovoko, in the Cannibal Islands, with their lip plugs and grass skirts or whatever. But this girl, there was something about her that went far beyond fashion.

She had the kind of beauty that punched you in the solar plexus and followed it up with a haymaker to the jaw. It wasn't her curves that got you, even though they were as luscious as a woman's curves can be. It was her irrepressible sweetness. Made a man want to belt the guy who hurt her.

Or worse.

When I first heard tell about her, I assumed it was just desire, good old-fashioned lust, that launched those thousand ships. But that was before I saw her. I'm not saying she did not inspire desire. Just watching her sway in silhouette across the window was enough to launch a mortar in a man's knickers. But it was the sweet languid innocence that got you. She was the most beautiful of roses, without any thorns to defend herself. Inexpressibly lovely. Helpless. Vulnerable. I could see why men left their families and their nations and set off to war in her defense.

Heck, if I'd had any ships, I would have launched 'em too.

She had a certain something that made a man want to help her, protect her, devote his life to her. But the dark side of desire is that same something made other men want to take her, use her, possess her.

And in this damned city, where there was no one really in charge, no governor, no police, no one to look out for the people the Wardens forgot, the strong did whatever they wanted. And the weak, they just suffered.

You'd be surprised how many periods of history were run along those lines. You'd be surprised how many folk long dead in pagan days just thought unkind fate or careless gods meant life was supposed to be like this. Here you start living with men who think brutality is normal, rubbing elbows with them. And on the days when you can't see the Moon or the city lights between the horns of the moon, you find yourself wondering where you took a wrong turn, wishing you could backtrack, and turn around again, and get back to where you'd been right.

I was sorry right away that I gave out a wolf whistle. She hadn't heard, but what was I, a steel worker? But then I quickly told myself she flaunted her talents for a living, so there was nothing wrong with my admiring her stock-in-trade, in eyeballing the merchandise. Nothing wrong at all, I told myself.

I tell myself a lot of things. But you knew that.

She stood, lightly on her feet, for a moment in front of that clear panel, and pointed the toes of her back leg as if she were reaching for something. Maybe she arched her back a little too much. Even from this far away, I could hear her giggle.

"Don't overdo it, doll," I muttered. "You don't want him to die of heart failure. Just get him to show himself."

I had told her to keep the window tuned open. On a cold night like this, she would want to keep warm, and she might forget.

Winter nights were never supposed to visit here. The Masters of Time, the Lords of Fate, the Chronocrats, the guys who can play card tricks with eons, centuries, histories and futures and human lives like stage magicians, whatever you want to call them, they are supposed to take care of all that.

They had many names. Some squires, servants or stoolies had seen them in the high places, stalking without noise through empty museums or across empty air in their strangely faceless, mirror-perfect armor of solidified time-energy, with their crowns of eternity-light and robes of entropy-mist. The servants whispered that the Masters of Time, whenever voices issued from their armor, or from the walls, or from nowhere, called themselves the Time Wardens, as if it were their job to protect time from being twisted and abused. As if they were not the main abusers.

Beneath the towers was a cloudscape of mists and fogs, a side effect of all the parachronic and anachronic energies emitted by the hidden machines of the Chronocrats. Too many changes to too many versions of the past had altered the location of land and sea. The photons wandering through overlapping fields of Schroedinger's Blur made solid objects look like phantoms, and phantoms look like clouds of mist. Maybe the towers rested on bedrock deep enough that no change of world history, no matter how far back, could touch it, or maybe the Time Wardens merely ordered gravity to stand still and then nailed the baseless towers in place. Could they do that? Why not? Gravity had something to do with Time, after all. I remember hearing that at a party.

At the moment, the mists below the towers were agitated, and smoky arms of cloudscape were climbing upward toward the black sky. In them you could see unfocused images of mountains and

islands and volcanoes, all flickering and shifting. That meant the
Continuum Winds were blowing. The disturbances could have been
caused by a careless Chronocrat meddling with his own past, or some
sort of disagreement, or duel, or war between two or more of them.

Except the Masters of Time don't fight wars—how could they?—
since all of them know how everything turns out. Or so I had been
told, back when I worked for those bastards.

Regardless of the reason why, the mist was rising, sending smoky
fingers reaching like greedy orphans toward the bright jewels of the
upper floors. And the temperature was dropping, because heat getting randomized, like photons losing their way, is another side effect
of a paradox poisoning the continuum.

The rising mist did not improve my mood. You can only patch a
garment so many times before it falls to pieces. But you knew that.

People don't die here. The Wardens take care of everything. I'd
been told that, too. Not that I was in the habit of believing everything I'm told.

Then I remembered that there was no final Old Gold waiting for
me. Some prophet from downstream had filched that last cigarette
from me, the bum. So it was back to bumming a puff from Queequeg's tomahawk, or putting the touch on Sir Walter Scott, who lived
two levels down. But I don't like pipes or cigars as much as ciggies.
They don't suit me.

On the other hand, the next time I had access to a working destiny
crystal, I could step backward through the calendar, or reach my
hand across last week and snatch it from my ghostward version. I
did not remember minding, not clearly, so younger-me would not
mind. Probably he would not.

The third member of the little party, Jack, had been posted in
front of the other entrance to this suite, the one Queequeg was not
watching. He kept walking back toward me, pretending he needed
to hear the plan again, but really just because he was nervous, and
wanted a chance to jaw.

Jack was fit, and looked young for his age, which I pegged somewhere between forty-five and fifty. He was dark-haired and slightly
squint-eyed, with a serious and strong-jawed face. He had a black
eye, but told me he didn't remember where he got it.

He was the client. Usually it was a mistake to bring the client out
on a job, but this time, I did not see what other choice I had.

"That's her. What do you think? Just as pretty in real life, eh?" he
said as he entered the silence field.

I had to give him points for remembering not to talk outside
the field. He had a broad-voweled Boston accent, the high-class
*Hahvahd* one. His breath was a cloud of cold steam.

"So that is Helen of Troy?" I said. "She don't look Greek to me."

"No. She is just one of them. One of the Helens of Troy. Helen
of Troys? What is the Plural of Helen of Troy?"

"Hellene," I guessed.

"Anyway, that one is mine. She's an actress. She can fool him. I'm
sure she can."

He was chattering because he was nervous. I wondered if he would
shut up if I said nothing.

Nope. He kept talking. "What are our chances, Mr. Frontino?"

He was dressed normally. I mean, what looked normal to
me: shoes, coat, tie, trenchcoat. You'd be surprised at how rare
shoes are in history. Boots and sandals for horsemen and higher
classes was the norm for most centuries, while everyone else went
barefoot.

No hat, though. If the men of my near future decide to stop
wearing the fedora, then they are crazy. It is not as if they do not
have hot sun and cold wind in the near future, not to mention bald
spots.

And what would you tip to a lady if a lady strolled by? And what
could you use to casually cover your gun hand if a cop strolled by?

Maybe there are no ladies in the future, but don't tell me there are
no cops. Even after all history is over and done with, and the Masters

of Time have retired to their golden city, there will still be cops. I know. I used to be one.

Jack was from the same timestream as me, same country, even the same century. By Metachronopolitan standards, that made us practically Siamese Twins. He was twenty years prophetic to me (or I was twenty years ghostly to him, same difference), but I could say things like: "Toto, I've a feeling we're not in Kansas any more" without either of us needing to have the artificial part of our memory blur in timeshift in order to insert a retroactive recollection of having had learned a language, or a lingo, we didn't previously remember having learned.

The Wardens can do things like that for their servants and serfs and slaves, as well as the people they keep as pets.

This tower was designated Special Prestige, which meant it had a double helping of golden light shining from it by day, more ambrosia in the air by night, more soaring music pouring from upper windows at odd hours, more gaiety and laughter. It also meant that if a slob with no prestige like me tried to step onto the high-arching bridges from the balcony of another tower, I would have found myself slipping through the diamond surface of the walkway and back five seconds to the moment before. Unless, that is, Jack, or someone else the Wardens took a fancy to, walked in with me.

"Our chances are good, aren't they, Mr. Frontino? You've done this before, right? You came highly recommended. Lucky Luciano said–" Then he must have realized his voice was creeping, note by note, into a higher pitch, and he clenched his teeth, hugging himself for warmth.

At this altitude, the tower was Greco-Roman. Higher up was European Ascendancy, Industrial Revolution, and rumors said there was even chamber dedicated to a Moonshot somewhere way high up, in the Twentieth Century level. At the moment we were low down, near the boundary where history turns into myth, but the tower was still plenty bright. Just not here, in this immediate section.

Behind me was the gently arching bridge leading across the nothingness to the shining tower of Babylon, where the folk and museum pieces came from the stream of time where the Greeks didn't win the pennant at Thermopylae, and it was the Persians who settled everywhere from the Mediterranean to the British Isles, discovered the jib sail, the printing press, gunpowder, and the New World. I didn't recognize any of the names that came after Cyrus, Xerxes and Darius.

But there is very little traffic between Babylonian and European Towers. There were no gardens nor cottages on this vast bridge as there were on so many others, nor were there rails, and most of the golden deck plates of solidified time energy were dark. There were even gaps in the understructure, gaping holes where plates were missing.

Why were there no rails on the bridge? Then again, why should there be? A Warden who reads in his future diary that he is due to fall off a bridge that day will just stay in bed. No, no one important cares if one of us little pawns falls off. The next time a Warden wants our services, he will simply make it so that we have not died and never did, as easily as he might ring for Jeeves the butler.

"Mr. K., there no such thing as chance in this town," I answered him. My throat was sore and my voice was a little rawer than it should have been. Blame the hooch. I could not get good whiskey here, and I sure as hell did not go out on nights like this, on a job like this, without one shot to warm me up, and another to steady my nerve. "There are only three ways this plays out. Either the guy is running blind and he is too dead to go back and warn himself, or nothing is going to happen because he looked ahead, saw the outcome, and decided not to show."

Jack had been some sort of big deal back in his home time. He was well-connected to the Old Money, and even better connected to the Mob, and he was an ace at politics. He was one of the most powerful men in the world in his day. But now he was just one more minor card in the deck of the Wardens. Here, even a historical somebody the Masters of Time liked to play with was still a nobody.

"Call me Jack." I don't think he was scared. He might have been trembling just from the cold. After all, the guy had been in the service. He had seen combat. You can always tell. It's in the look in the eyes, the set of the shoulders.

"I appreciate the gesture, sir. I do." I said patiently. "But you're a client of mine, and if Beidler or Jefferson gets wind of this, or Alexander the Great... if there is any investigation, I never knew you. A man's got to watch his own back. I do what I am hired to."

"I understand that. But if you are not on a first name basis with a man who is pulling a—is doing a—I mean, doing a job for you–"

Then again, maybe it was not the cold making him shiver. Shooting a man in the enemy uniform in a hot war when he is shooting at you, that is not the same as gunning down a guy in cold blood who dresses like you.

"It's not homicide," I said flatly, cutting him off.

"Whatever you want to call it," he said with a shrug. "Just so it gets done."

His voice was normally charming, smooth, rich-toned. Now it was colder than the mists closing in. It was the voice of a judge pronouncing a death sentence, or a commander-in-chief sending brave young men to their deaths.

"No, sir," I said. "I mean that it really will not be homicide. I am going to wait until she's in actual danger. Slaying a man in self defense or defense of others is justified. Killing him for the sake of revenge is not."

"Not even revenge for rape? Not even for that?"

Maybe the cold was giving him the shakes. Maybe he was scared. Or maybe he was shaking with rage.

I shrugged. Don't get me wrong. I felt for the guy. I would have done the same thing in his shoes. Heck, I once killed a man for beating a girl. (I would have just broke a finger or two if he had not pulled a knife. I took it out of his hand and left it in his eye.) Girls are special. You are supposed to take care of girls. Defend them. I get it. I understand.

But I got my principles. They aren't the best principles in the world. In fact, they are pretty shabby. Someday I should take them out of hock, polish them up. But they are what I got. They are all I got.

Killing a man in cold blood, no. I won't do it. Killing a man attacking a girl in her bedroom in cold blood, you bet. Glad to.

Because if you rescue Helen of Troy, that makes you a hero, and old Homer will sing a song about you.

Old Homer lives directly below me, off the waste chute in the hall, and sometimes I bring him doughnuts, if I can steal them from the Great War commissary, which is two floors up. He sang a mighty song for Little John when John saved Helen from Paris of Troy by cracking the kid's spine with a quarterstaff. From the gut-side, I should mention.

And Homer sang a mighty song for William "Big Bill" Dwyer when Bill saved another version of Helen, who was from a parallel timeline where she was married to Theseus of Athens before being carried off by Menelaus of Sparta. The Spartan king ended up with a longshoreman's hook through his soft parts. Little John was one of Robin Hood's gang, and a cutpurse, and Big Bill had been a stevedore before he turned to rum-running and hockey.

I didn't want to be a hero. Dangerous work. Lousy pay. But it is better than being a murderer, and I wouldn't have minded that song.

Beside, Judge Roy Bean said he would buy a drink at the Stag's Head for anyone Homer sings about. Homer gets free drinks himself for singing about a guy named Demodocus.

"I will rescue her," I said. "And I will kill him in the act if he attacks her. And smile while I do it. But I will not assassinate anyone."

Jack was silent for a moment, his eyes cast down. He was looking at the baseball bat I had tucked under my elbow. My other weapon, my Special, was holstered under my armpit. I also had a switchblade in my pocket, giving me three weapons.

"That's only two," said Jack.

"Two what?" I said, surprised. For a moment I was wondering if he knew I was counting up the number of guys who killed people for Helen. Or counting my weapons.

"Outcomes. Three outcomes." He said. "But you only mentioned two. What is the third?"

"The third outcome is that he saw what is going to happen and likes the way it turned out. That means he brings the Tin Wood-man."

"The what?"

"A mechanical man. Like Elektro from the New York World's Fair. A robot. It can timeshift up to five minutes, and it will always be where it needs to be before you can. Bullets and rays and stuff bounce off its armor, unless you hit it in a joint, because the armor is made out of solid time-stuff like the tower walls. The one weakness it has is that whatever is not listed as a weapon in its orders, it ignores. Some of them are more sophisticated than others."

"Others? Is there more than one?"

"Maybe. Maybe not. It might be the same one from different moments in time. And it's armed. It carries an ax. It can step forward or back in time through a five-minute range, until it finds the one split-second you are off-balance or not looking. It can take all the time in the world and try again as often as it likes. It takes trophies too. It chops off the heads and stores them inside its skull, which is hollow and made of glass like a fishbowl, so that everyone can see who it killed last."

"Grisly. Sounds like something from your Man's island."

"He's not my Man."

"What?"

"Quickwig." (That's not his name, but it's as close as us guys from the Bronx can say it.) "He's doing me a favor out of the benevolence of his big heart. It's not like I got anything to swap him for. Besides, he is a prince. Back in his day."

Jack nodded. He knew the feeling.

"So Quickwig outranks me," I said.

"He does not seem like the type who does your kind of work."

"The first time I met Quickwig, we were rooming together. We had to share a bed, because of the crowding. He came at me with his harpoon and I was too slow with my pistol. I had to wrestle him. He broke my neck, and the Time Wardens brought me back to life. So I decided we had to be friends. I replayed the scene and gave him the bed this time, and bowed politely to his little fetish named Yojo, and once Yojo said I was Jake, everything was copacetic."

"Sounds like a good man to have in your corner."

"He is. Even though he eats people."

Jack shivered again. "You come from the Twentieth Century. You know modern life has a price. The noble savage is closer to unspoiled Eden than we are."

"Don't be a jerk, sir, if you don't mind my saying so. Every sorry last one of us is just as far from Eden as everyone else." I said. The words tasted bitter in my mouth. I turned my head and spat over the railing. The wad of spittle arced down into the mist, lost interest in gravity, and dissolved.

"In any case, the beheading habit allows the Tin Man to make kill-identifications easier back at the station. And if there is a Warden at the station, sometimes he will backdate the Tin Man, so it when you suddenly find it standing next to you with an axe, you can see your own bloody head, with a surprised and stupid look of shock, staring out from inside the hollow glass helmet of the machine. At least, I think the Tin Woodman is a machine."

"You mean you don't know?"

"Quickwig says the Tin Woodman is a hobgoblin called Talamaur. They suck life from the dying and eat the hearts of healthy men when they sleep. Who can say his guess is not closer to the horseshoe stake of truth than mine?"

"Toto, I've a feeling we're not in Kansas any more," said Jack sourly. "So what happens if he has a Tin Man with him?"

"Then the third outcome is a sure thing."

"What's that?"

"If he shows up with a Tin Woodman, I am already dead."

At that moment, a beautiful, softly lilting song, half-breathless, half-panting and all-purring, came from the window. She was singing. It sounded so much like a love song, a song of erotic passion, that I did not actually catch the words.

When I did, I laughed. She really was pulling out all the stops, wasn't she?

*Happy birthday to you,*
*Happy birthday to you-uu*
*Happy birthday-yy*
*Mister President...*

And then the girl let out a scream like the shriek of a bird of prey. She had the trained voice of a singer and an actress who could hit the high notes loud enough to hear in the cheap seats, and she certainly was built like she had the excess lung capacity.

There were shadows in the semi-transparent window. For a moment, I thought it was two figures, the girl and her attacker come back for seconds. And then I laughed with the feeling that only cops who work for Time Wardens know, a feeling of relief, because you remember seeing the date on the headstone of the guy who just drew a knife and is coming for you.

It is like wearing the armor of the inevitable. It is like getting a big wet sloppy kiss from Lady Fate. Because you know, beyond any shadow of the doubt, that *he* is a dead man, not you.

Then I stopped laughing.

A bulky figure in a trenchcoat and a wide-brimmed slouch hat stepped out of the shower stall, of all places, and even with the window half dim, I could see the bathroom lights shining between the upturned collar and the downturned hat brim, right through the glass of his empty head. So I knew I was the dead man.

My head was not propped inside the machine-man's glass skull, which meant I would die by a method that destroyed the whole body, a method that left no corpse. You know what that means in this city.

I looked down at my gun, which was now in my hand. It was a Police Special. What I held in my fist was just the aiming unit, the emission aperture and the firing controls. The real weapon was the size of a warehouse sitting in a null-time vacuole in the fourth-and-a-half dimension, halfway past next Tuesday or somewhere beyond the second star to the right, with atomic piles and dynamos and batteries of big guns and futuristic zap-rays and a whole arsenal of various brands of death and maiming and unhappiness. It could blow a hole in the Moon or pick the left wing off a housefly landing on the Washington Monument from the Empire State Building, and never mind the curvature of the Earth or the prevailing winds. It was that good.

Now, it was useless. The Tin Woodman was programmed to identify it as a weapon. No matter what I did with it, the action would be counteracted before I fired.

There were tremors of cold shivering through my fingers, and I saw little blurry patches of mist clinging to my fingers. A time paradox. A decision point.

This was a moment where I either turned and ran, like Oedipus trying to run away from his cursed life, or I could go in and die like a Kamikaze pilot, a sacrifice to destiny.

"Banzai!"

I ran up the nearer ramp toward the girl and sprinted toward my death.

I'd had a pretty good life, I guess. I had no complaints.

Strike that. My life stank like an incontinent skunk pie sandwich with no mustard, if one of the slices was the crusty heel no one likes to eat, and I had loads of complaints.

As I ran, I let go of my Special, and the gun used its tractor field to jump like a fish and slide back into my armpit holster. With the same motion, I brought the baseball bat I was carrying to my shoulder. Joe DiMaggio had given it to me. The Yankee Clipper. Signed it, too, with a hot engraver's pen. It was my prize possession.

Jack was ahead of me. Unlike me, he had not hesitated. My face felt hot for the first time that night as I ran after him, trying to catch up to him. I was blushing for shame. Damn me if I would let a client go into harm's way first!

Out of the corner of my eye, I saw Queequeg's shadow move between me and the doorway to the far ramp, the other entrance. In his bare feet, he was surprisingly quiet and surprisingly swift. His deadly harpoon, which can kill a mammal much bigger than a man, was held lightly at his shoulder. His top hat was resting carefully behind him on the balcony deck, upon the spot where he had been posted, so it would not get mussed.

I followed Jack. Queequeg could handle himself. My ears popped as I passed through whatever unseen forcefield or abracadabra magic, or whatever it was that stretched across the threshold to the tower and allowed the Wardens to keep the weather outside without the need for a physical door.

And, no, we did not bounce off the force field or end up five seconds in the past. Not that there was any way to find out what was off-limits until the moment after you find yourself in the moment before, looking stupid. There are no leases in the City, since the Masters of Time own everything, but there are rosters and quartermasters and people with prestige among the Swell Set. And then there were people with pull and those with favors to call in among the Not So Swell. And there were tough guys with tougher reputations to maintain among the Really Not Swell At All. Whatever the quartermaster or the ward boss assigned, you didn't take, but you swapped to someone who had something you liked better, or you gave him your marker. So everyone knew who really owned what, and who owed who, but nothing was written down.

This was Jack's apartment. He did not live there, and his name was not on the ward roster, but he had prestige, and his lieutenants had pull, and his boys had reputations, so it was for all intents and purposes his.

Jack was pelting up the ramp. He reached the upper corridor. It was brighter in here, all glowing gold walls and display cases like a museum. I could see the pistol in his hand, a footlong length of polished and gilded wood and lustrous pewter. It was a flintlock, or it looked like one. I had not inspected it very closely when I obtained it from Aaron Burr late yesterday, in return for forgetting his past. It had been just before the evening horserace and evening riot at the hippodrome (Bucephalus had bested Marengo in the last race, and was running against Traveller, and odds were running twelve to seven for Lee's horse.) I barely had time before evening curfew to get from the riot to Jack, and no time to instruct him.

Had Jack even loaded the pistol? Did he know how? I did not remember whether I had told him how to load and hold it, not to assume pistols of that type would stay loaded. Inwardly, I cursed myself. It is that kind of small mistake, not double-checking the details, that gets men killed. But it was too late.

She screamed again. Jack had seen too many movies, because he raised his foot and kicked at the door panel leading into the bedroom of the suite. He ended up on his backside staring at the glowing gold ceiling.

I turned off the silence field and said: "Allow me."

My gun leaped into my hand from the holster, projected an aiming beam, then launched a missile made of white-hot plasma instead of old-fashioned metal. The gun emitted a magnetic force field shaped like a tube to guide the missile to the target, then designed and built an invisible set of braces and baffles out of nucleonic energy-tension to suppress the explosion within a five-foot radius. Then the gun focused a time distortion hole on the spot to sweep the wreckage of the door panels and part of the wall sideways out of the continuum, into the non-being between timestreams, as the missile plasma ruptured and made a miniature version of a sun.

So, not only was Jack and half the planet not killed, all he saw was a perfect circle-shaped hole appear in the wooden wall. Also, a perfect vacuum-globe appeared in the air in front of him, then imploded with a bang. I guess nature abhorred it, since it immediately vanished and was replaced by a shockwave that pulled Jack forward and hurled him into the bedroom.

I holstered my gun, gripped the bat in both hands and followed him at a less hectic pace.

It was like stepping into a Museum diorama tuned to the Mid-Twentieth Century, coastal North America. The original suite had been one large chamber made of invulnerable gold walls. Now, the inside had been portioned off into human-sized rooms by walls of wood and plaster, and apportioned with furniture and appliances like you might see in a rich man's home. Since I did not often get invited into wealthy drawing rooms, the place looked like something I had only seen in motion pictures. Only everything was in color.

There were cut crystal sets, ornaments on marble stands, a coffee table, a couch, a big silk-covered bed to one side, a door to the bathroom to the other, a bar or miniature kitchen stocked with electronic wonder gizmos, and lots of carpet underfoot. Only the far wall, the one with the man-high window in it, was gold. Drapes were hung across it to block the golden glow from outside. And there was a chandelier overhead, to give light because the glow was blocked. This is the kind of useless extravagance that only the people the Wardens really, really like get to enjoy. Jack was not one of the middle ranks of the mortals of Metachronopolis. He was from the tip-top, the flaky upper crust. He was one of the guys the Wardens let play with their toys.

By fate or chance or cosmic design, Jack landed on top of the guy in the long black cloak—I kid you not, the target was dressed like a comic opera villain from the Silent pictures of last decade—just as the guy tore the towel off the girl.

No sooner had Jack landed than he was kneeling on the guy's arms, punching him in the face with one fist, and strangling him with the other hand. Blood was streaming from the guy's nose, into his gray beard and his thin gray hair.

The bearded face was wrinkled. The girl's attacker was an old man.

My guess was late sixties, so he was perhaps twenty or thirty years older than Jack. And it was not an opera cape that he was wearing. It was a self-heating thermocloak from the Twenty-First Century, the thing they use in hospitals to medicate patients and keep their hearts working. So, he was not only old, he was decrepit. You had to wonder where he found the juice to get his Walla Walla Washington to stand up and salute.

A walking stick had fallen from his thin, veiny hand. It did not look like the sort of stick that rich men carry to show that they don't need to muss their hands with work. It looked like the type old men lean on because their legs are weak. At the top of the stick was a gold knob. My gun beeped at me and told me the knob was producing a time distortion effect, but it only had a nine-inch range. He had to be holding it for it to work, so it was no source of danger at the moment.

Horrid gargling noises were coming from the old man as Jack squeezed his throat.

The Tin Woodman turned toward me. Not *turn*, exactly. It blinked from facing away from me to facing toward me, its shoulders hunched and its gauntlets raised. It was holding a long-handled executioner's axe; a half-moon of sharpened metal shining like brass formed the business end with a spike sticking out the other way.

The monster looked like a freakish cross between the headless horseman from Sleepy Hollow, the guy who knows what evil lurks

in the hearts of men from that radio program, and beneath that, a
knight from Avalon in plate armor of purest gold. There was nothing
but a fishbowl glint between its hat and its trenchcoat collar.

Behind it, through an open door, I could see the glass door of the
shower stall, of the sort you might see in a fancy New York hotel.
There was a destiny crystal plate hidden in the glass door. How
long ago it had been planted there? The old man could have done it
decades in the past, or even centuries. My plan of watching the place
from outside had been as futile as Mr. A Square of Flatland trying
to sneak up on the Sphere of Spaceland by hiding carefully behind a
line.

How come I was still alive? In the same blink it had taken the Tin
Man to turn to face me, he could have blinked across the room and
chopped my head off, or blinked back four minutes, and attacked
me from behind as I ran up the ramp.

Then I realized that the Tin Man had not been given clear instructions. My attack on the door panel had not been an attack on his
master. It did not count.

And Jack had been thrown by accident on top of the old man. A
human body is not necessarily a lethal weapon. The Tin Man was
not smart enough to understand that Jack was strangling the old man.
The old man could not speak and order the attack because Jack was
crushing his windpipe.

Not that anyone could have heard anything anyway. The most
beautiful girl in history was standing in the middle of the room,
blond and pink and quivering with fear, naked as a jaybird, round
and delicious as a peach.

Actually, she was not a blond, not a natural one anyhow, but she
was so perfect in her proportions and poise that I actually took my
eyes off the Tin Man—who was certain to kill me—to stare at her.
Only for a moment, of course. But if that is the last thing in the
life you are to see, what better to stare at? She was screaming loud
enough to peel paint off the walls.

Jack shouted: "Now! Frontino! Smash his face! Break his skull! Hit him!"

The Tin Man did not retroactively decapitate me just yet. Maybe it was programmed to regard a baseball bat as equipment for a game and not a deadly weapon.

What did I have to lose? I was dead anyway. I took one last look at the girl to remind myself of what I was fighting for. Then I stepped forward and raised the baseball bat overhead in both hands...

There was a flick of misty nonexistence for a second and then I was in a version of the scene where the Tin Man was standing between me and the old man, and my bat bounced harmlessly off a dark overcoat sleeve covering an upraised arm of gold.

I should explain: I have a hardened memory. It is a rare trait, apparently found, or so I was told, in the remote ancestors of those who will someday be Time Wardens. It allows me to remember if someone changes my past. I can remember both versions as easily as if one were real and one were imaginary. Deja vu is a weaker edition of the same effect. Anyone might have the ability, but if you never cross paths with a time traveler who changes your past, how would you ever know? Most people who are brought to this city have hardened memory in some form, some stronger than others.

So I remembered both the original version where the Tin Man crossed the room by walking slowly until he stood between me and the old man and then blurred backward a few seconds in the time direction as well as the revised version where he appeared in an eyeblink right in front of me.

But I did not remember a version where I smashed in the old man's head. In the original version, the Tin Woodman was simply not moving fast enough to stop me. I stopped me, not him. Jack had learned to one side as he grasped the old man's neck in both hands, to provide me a clear target. Because Jack's hands were pinning the white beard down, I saw the old man's face clearly enough to see what he would have looked like if he were clean-shaven.

Meanwhile, in this version, the Tin Man was between me and the two men on the floor, so I stepped quickly back and raised my bat as if to bunt, hoping to parry the axe if Tin Man swung.

There was a blur of mist around its axe, and my pistol's paradox alarm went off. At the same time I remembered the sensation of the axe biting into my neck from behind and the tingling sensation of my pistol erecting a skintight force nimbus over my body.

You see, my gun was every bit as smart as the Tin Man. It may have been designed by the same Time Warden engineers, for all I knew. The axe rebounded from an invisible collar of force lines that were swirling around my neck.

Suddenly the Tin Man was between me and the door—or, rather the hole—leading out. We were now in a version of the scene where the Tin Man had decided not to take a swing at me. Instead, my baseball bat had been cut in half and the palms of my hands were stinging. So were my eyes. Yes, I teared up. Not from the pain in my hands or the shock in my arms, but because an axe had just smashed through my favorite baseball bat. My Joe DiMaggio bat!

I wanted to swear, but there was a very, very attractive lady in the room. I shouted at the old man. "I should have killed you! Smashed your damn—sorry—*darned* skull into pieces!"

Why hadn't I? Because I had seen his face. And no, it wasn't my face, if that is what you are thinking.

At that moment, the girl stopped screaming. She grabbed the towel around her head, and tucked it not very effectively around her abundant curve as she called out to Jack in a whisper of horror. "That is the man who attacked me last week. It's him! Mr. President! Won't you help me? Don't let him hurt me again!" She sounded as innocent as a lamb and as breathless as a bride caught up in the rapture of her first nuptial night. A hard combination to pull off.

What a voice! I promised myself never to wash my ears again.

Jack said: "Run, Norma Jean! Run!"

The girl turned to the broken wall which had once held the door out, but the Tin Man stood in the way.

Jack's grip had slackened. The old man managed to gasp out a word. "P-protect!"

The command was enough. The world blinked. The Tin Man was helping the Old Man sit up and Jack had been flung like a rag doll all the way across the coffee table. He hit the far wall with a noise like a gong. He had not been decapitated. That explained a lot. The Tin Man must have known that killing Jack would create a paradox.

I saw Aaron Burr's gun lying right at my feet. I stooped, picked it up, and looked at it. My pistol automatically scans and analyzes potential threats, and it can insert into my memory-chain the memory of having had given me a read out.

Aaron Burr was a cheat. The inside of the flintlock had been replaced with newer technology and contained a magazine of real bullets complete with sabot and primer caps, cleverly hidden in the stock, and a rifled barrel. The bullets were made of a smart metal designed to deform on impact, so that anyone digging open the wound later would find nothing but a pistol ball. The thing even had microminiaturized ranging and aiming circuits. I'd always wondered how Hamilton lost that duel. He was the better shot, and had won each time the Time Wardens made the two weary, ever-resurrected men replay that fatal scene.

I tossed the dueling pistol to the girl. "Don't point it at the old man until five minutes from now, after I lure the Tin Man away. There is a timer in the action. When it rings, shoot him. Twice in the chest, once in the head. Hold it in both hands, with your arms straight. Just take a breath, let it out, and squeeze the trigger slowly."

She said, "I am not sure I can... do that. I couldn't even butcher chickens back home."

Of course. If Helen of Troy were the kind of dame who could shoot a man without turning green, would she be abducted even once? Some girls are born girlish. You cannot blame them. Much.

"Ma'am, this is the man who attacked you, isn't it?" I spoke in my coldest voice.

Her lips quivered and she did not answer.

The old man had climbed to his knees. He looked up and looked at her with such hunger that it sickened me. His voice was strong for an old guy, but his words were weary. "Life is a broad way and a banquet when you are young, and every sunrise is promises and hopes. When you are old, life is narrow and crooked and cramped, and all your friends are dead, and you have no tomorrow to talk about, and all you have is your memories."

The old man tried to rise to his feet but he was too weak. He groped for his cane, with a hand that looked like a blind albino spider crawling, but it was out of reach. So the old man continued to kneel, the Tin Man's metal hands holding him up.

His laugh was a cracked wheezing sound like an accordion with a hole in it. "But if you are friends with a Time Warden, then your memories are not out of your reach, are they? Why resist temptation, if the powers that rule eternity give you your dearest, darkest heart's desire?"

The girl shivered. The girl shivered. "That's his voice. He talked a lot in my ear. He's a talker. It's him. Why do I have to kill him? Why not you? What are men for? What good are you?"

There were wisps of mist clinging to the corners of the chamber, now. Too many paradoxes, too many versions. There had already been at least half a dozen time splits here already.

I said to her, "Just think of what it felt like when he attacked you, and how nothing seemed safe or normal or human to you afterward. Squeeze the trigger slowly. He'll get shot."

The time splits so far were not enough to account for this much mist. There had to be at least one more source of paradox here. I turned my eyes left and right, but did not see anything out of place. I took a step forward, picked up the Old Man's walking stick, and chucked it through the bathroom doorway. I did not hear it ring against the crystal panel of the shower stall door, nor clatter against the ceramic tile. Bingo. A polarized silence field, like my own. Sound could enter the bathroom, but not leave. A useful thing to bring to a place where there is a secret entrance, because no one will hear you as you arrive.

The old man sneered wearily. "I won't. Be shot, I mean. An automaton from the Fortieth Century is my bodyguard. No bullet can hit me."

Without bothering to answer, I turned and pointed at the bathroom door. The Tin Man was stupid. Its master's only escape was not on its automatic defense list. I got the shot off before the old man could say another word. Another shape of momentary non-being flicked into non-existence, but I had tuned it to affect the shower door and nothing else. I did not break the mirror or smash the toilet or harm anyone hiding in the bathtub. The shower door-shaped square of nothing collapsed like a popped balloon, but thanks to the silence field, this time there was no imploding clap of thunder. The old man, from his position in the bedroom, probably did not even know that I had fired, or at what.

None of my weapons could hurt a destiny crystal, of course. But the bathroom shower door, utterly unhurt, was now drifting somewhere in the mists between the time lines, beyond the reach of anyone.

The mist closes off all destiny crystal. The crystal is just an anchor point for a conduit, like a miniature spacetime continuum, that the Wardens erect between two points up and down the time stream. Or, rather, the time delta, since there are many branching paths. When destiny crystal is adjusted for photons, you can see images. Crystal ball stuff. Open it a little more, you can get sounds and smells and maybe reach an arm through. Open all the way, and it is a door.

But you cannot open them in the mist. The mist is what happens when you have too many low probability events, causeless effects or effectless causes, all piled up in one spot. Reality there is weak. There is nothing to to which the anchor point can be attached.

With the glass door gone, I was no longer worried about the old man sending any later-time version of himself, or a dozen versions of Tin Man, once a year on his birthday to relive the happy moment when he saw my head chopped off. And now there was no escape for him.

Experimentally, I pointed my pistol at the old man and pulled the trigger. My shot tore the black trenchcoat and bounced off the golden chestplate of the Tin Man, who blinked in the way as if he had always been standing there. Again, my neck and neck bones ached from the hardened memory of the decapitation that retroactively took place, and from the choking sensation of my nimbus retroactively blocking the blow.

The old man said, "Mister Frontino, you do not survive the evening. I've looked ahead. I have seen you fall. I have already won. Game, set and match!" He smirked at me. "You are about to run. Leaving me alone with her."

I smirked right back. He was a good smirker, but I was better. "But did you watch after that?"

He looked shocked. "What do you take me for? A voyeur?"

Jack shouted at me, "What are you doing? Shoot him! He is not a Time Warden! He can die! Shoot him!"

Much to his surprise, I pointed my pistol at Jack.

"This is your last chance, Mr. K.! Give up the girl. Swear her off, now and forever and back through your past, and one of the three of you can walk out of here alive!"

The old man burst out laughing. "You've got to be kidding," he wheezed.

He had a point. I mean, the girl was right here, the all-time winner of history's beauty contest. I could smell her fresh from the shower, and even with all that was going on, I could not get my mind off her. That was just from seeing her for a minute or so. I did not have years of her burned into my life and memory. Would I be willing to give up the girl with the face that launched a thousand ships if she had once been mine?

The answer came with the next blur of mist. Another decision point. But the old man had not vanished. No one was giving up anything. Instead there was another remembered sensation of pain at my neck. That confirmed it for me. The old man was protecting Jack too.

I pulled the trigger. The Tin Man blinked in between me and Jack, and the ricochet set the couch on fire. Then there was another blur, and in this version the Tin Man caught the ricochet in the cupped palm of its gauntlets as it rebounded from its chest armor. It could stop me from hurting anything, directly or indirectly.

"Run, Jack," I told him quietly. "Run to Babylon."

Jack turned and leaped through the hole in the wall where the door had been. The Tin Man was not programmed to stop him. But when I followed and shot Jack in the back, well, there had to be a version where Tin Man blinked in the way and deflected my bolt with his axe.

The Tin Man and I were stalemated. It would not hurt me, and I could not hurt it, not with anything it recognized as a weapon. Tin Man could not stop me from shooting, but could stop me from killing Jack.

A few minutes later the three of us were running across the darkened bridge toward the Babylon tower, I had dialed my hand weapon to a flamethrower and high-energy laser setting, so that deathrays and masses of flaming jellied gasoline were washing and rolling every which way. Tin Man was blinking through every version of the scene so quickly, and shattering the timestream into smaller and smaller fractions, that the mist under our feet grew thicker and angrier, and the cold got colder, and finally, it started to snow.

Picture a bridge made of slippery golden crystal metal, too dark for human eyes to see, coated with frost and falling snow and new ice and pools of burning petrol melting a layer of water beneath the ice. And there were gaps in the surface underfoot which no Warden bothered to order repaired, even assuming anyone in this city knew how to repair this stuff. Or assuming anyone knew who built it. The Wardens say they built it, but you can't believe everything you are told.

Normally a robot that can step backward through time cannot slip and fall. Nor can a man whom the robot can easily dodge tackle it. But a harpoonist with a steady hand and the best eye in the Pacific Ocean, a dark prince in a tall hat, who stands silently on a balcony overhead and watches like a hawk, well, he can throw his harpoon straight and true into the glass skull that is the monster's only weak spot.

It did not kill the Tin Man. How could it? It was just a machine. The glass skull was merely a hood ornament. Something to scare its victims.

But it had a collar and heavy clamps to hold its trophy skulls in place. The razor-sharp harpoon could not penetrate on the gold null-time substance of the armor. But the toggle barbs in the shaft could catch the protrusions inside the metal neckring of the machine, and lodge the harpoon fast as if it had been hammered in.

The Tin Man would have dodged a spear or a lance or a javelin, stepped back in time, and decapitated the spearman. But the circuits in my pistol did not recognize a whaler's harpoon as a weapon. I found that out the day I met Queequeg the first time. And whoever had programmed the Tin Man made the same mistake.

Now, you may ask, why did Tin Man not simply step backward in time and step to one side of the predicted flightpath of the harpoon? You may have noticed how often I let the Tin Man hit me in the neck. You may have noticed that the damned thing did not learn. It was not programmed to update its programming. It kept trying to decapitate me because that was what it was ordered to do.

There were no loopholes, no exceptions, no if's and's or but's. When the target (me) was holding a weapon that threatened its client (in this case, Jack) and was in the position to be struck in the neck by the Tin Man's axe, then, as predictably as loaded dice rolling a lucky seven, the Tin Man had to move to that position and take that swing.

It was not programmed to watch its step and protect itself, because what could hurt it through its ultra-invulnerable time-null armor? And if it was hurt, so what? Just get the Warden to replay the scene and change the ending.

So when I saw the harpoon enter the glass skull and lodge there, I realized what I had to do next (next from my point of view), to explain why the Tin Man would not in a moment from now (or, from its point of view, just a moment ago) retroactively dodge Queequeg's harpoon strike.

I took my gun in my teeth with autogyroscopic aiming circuit turned on, so the barrel spun this way and that like the nose of a tapir, always keeping an aiming laser pointed at Jack. Then I rushed towards the Tin Man and tackled him.

Queequeg heaved on the harpoon line with the strength a man gets from wrestling whales, and he yanked Tin Man off the slippery metal frost-coated bridge deck.

Our trenchcoats flapped and fluttered, and my hat flew off, as over the side we went.

It was programmed to keep decapitating the threat. As we fell, the Tin Man reversed its grip on the axe and made a motion like a man swatting a fly on his face. And then it did it again, and again, because Tin Man was not ordered to save itself from danger. It was programmed to hit me. And the only place it could hit me, if I were off the bridge, was likewise off the bridge.

I hope you can follow this Celtic knot of cause and effect here. If I hadn't grabbed the machine that can dodge any grab, the machine would not have stood still and let itself get harpooned with the harpoon, because then my grab would have missed. And it permitted me to grab it, it could not do otherwise, because with my arms around it, it could hit me, and if it had dodged, it could not.

We were in plunging towards the mists. With gun still clenched in my teeth like a pirate's cutlass, I seized the harpoon line with both hands and both legs and managed to snag it. Then, with one hand and two legs still clutching the line, I drew my switchblade with my free hand, flicked it open and reached for the loop between me and the Tin Man. Just then the line went taut, the wind was knocked out of me, and the switchblade went spiraling downward into the mists of oblivion.

Dammit! The day Gavrilo Princip was hanged in the stairwell of the Royal Exile Diner, where Franz Ferdinand of Austria worked as a busboy, Franz wept for joy into his apron, but he had nothing to give me. So John X. Beidler, who ran the northwest Vigilance Committee, let me keep the assassin's switchblade knife. First my bat, now this. It was my day for losing things

I put one hand on the line above the harpoon head, and had my feet kicking and slipping on the golden shoulders and ripped trenchcoat of the Tin Man.

Above us, through the swimming blur of intervening mists, I saw Jack, staring over the side of the bridge in awe and fear.

Jack's head jerked up and disappeared when the girl screamed again, and I also, very dimly, heard the timer I'd set in Aaron Burr's pistol go off. Had it been five minutes already? It felt more like five years.

But no shot rang out. Some people are just too kind-hearted for their own good. Or too soft-headed.

There was only one thing left to do. I put my head down so that the harpoon line was clamped between my chin and my breastbone. I felt the pain in my neck as the machine reached up and swung his axe at me, severing the line which was the only thing preventing his heavy and utterly invulnerable body from plummeting into the bottomless, smoky white nothingness below.

*Goodbye, Tin Man. I think I'll miss you least of all.* I wish that its engineer would have programmed the damned thing with a voice circuit, so that I could have heard it go *Aaaeeiiii!* as it plunged into oblivion. Design flaw, if you ask me. Anyway, that was one pain in the neck gone.

"Down, boy," I muttered. And my gun magnetically walked down my chest into my holster, folded itself up, and slid inside for a nap.

Getting back onto the bridge did not take as long as it seemed, because Queequeg was hauling me up even faster than I was climbing the line, so before I knew it, I was above the mist surface. Then a strong dark hand with thick calluses and grimy nails was reaching down and plucking me up as easily as I might have plucked up a kitten drowning in a toilet bowl.

"You jump. What for? No life no more for you?" Queequeg squinted and hid a smile.

"Nope. I wasn't committing suicide. The man we're hunting saw me in a destiny glass. A prophecy. But he did not say he saw me die. He only said he saw me fall. He could not see what happened after I fell into the mist, because destiny glasses can't see through the mist. That's why he thought the outcome was safe, so why he entered the scene."

Queequeg stepped over and carefully picked up his top hat, brushed it fastidiously, and placed in on his head, raising his chin with princely pride. "Enemy, he falls too. Not a good death. Nothing to eat."

"Which enemy?"

"Talamaur." He pointed toward the mist with a jerk of his chin.

"You can't eat metal. You would have broken your teeth."

"Yojo, he eat spirit. No eat metal." Queequeg looked at the severed end of his line in his hand where there hung the conspicuous absence of his best harpoon. He grimaced stoically, and began winding up the slack around his elbow in rapid, practiced motions. "Yojo, he says I save you enough for one day."

"Am I still in danger?"

"Yojo smells death. Death soon comes. Man we hunt, you say he looks. Sees future. Sees what comes. He sees you fall down into mist. Yes?"

"Yes."

He poked me in the chest with a thick, dark forefinger. His finger felt like an iron poker. "Then why it is he sees not you climb out of mist? He dies. He sees he dies, yes? But if he sees, how it is he dies?"

He turned and walked away into the gloom.

"Quickwig! What about the hunt? I said you would feast after we get him!"

A hollow laugh answered me. "Eat flesh, not mist."

You are probably wondering why I was not rushing back to save the girl I'd left alone with the lecherous old man. But I'd lived too long in the city beyond Time to be in a hurry. You see, I figured it was a done deal. If I was not the dead man, then he must be the dead man. No matter what happened, the old man was not making it out of this scene alive. Sooner or later, this was the end for him.

So I did not run, I strolled back up the ramp, through the hole in the wall, and into the room with the hole in the bathroom.

The girl was there. She had draped the silk sheet from the bed around her body, making it look as if she was wearing a long flowing toga. She was sitting on the edge of the bed and slowly getting to her feet. Her eyes were half-lidded, as if she had just been hit with a stun ray. Or maybe that was just the natural cast of her features.

And Jack was there, with Aaron Burr's cheater gun in his hand. The alarm was still ringing. Ding, ding, ding, ding. The girl was moaning, sobbing, which somehow she still managed to make sound alluring. And Jack was panting as if he had just run a race.

The old man was on the ground at Jack's feet, gasping and unable to speak, trying to hold his thin and trembling hands over his face and stomach and groin all at the same time. He had the walking stick, but he was not using it to block the blows or strike back. In fact, he was curled around it as if trying to protect it.

"Any last words?" said Jack. The old man was out of breath, and could not speak. He just whimpered.

"It's not a good shoot, Mr. K." I said. "He isn't placing anyone in immediate threat of life or limb now. This isn't self-defense."

Jack gave me a look of hatred. "You going to stop me, flatfoot?"

"Hell, no. You went to a lot of trouble, more than you remember, to set up this scenario. I don't care about him and I sure as hell don't care about you. How old are you, Jack? You look about fifty. You were supposed to die at forty-six. Any time you lived here was extra time. And here you are, throwing it away."

"Mr. President, don't you understand what he's saying?" the girl said anxiously. "Don't shoot him! Please don't!"

The old man had gotten his breath back, and he had a strangely calm look on his face. A look of resignation. Of defeat.

But in his eyes there gleamed an eerie hate-filled look of victory.

Jack pulled the trigger. The noise felt like a hammer driving a spike into my ear. The gun barrel was less then two feet from the old man's head, so his skull exploded like a watermelon, and the carpet was transformed into the floor of your local butcher shop, the one in the back room that no customer ever sees. The smell of blood and cordite did to my nose what the deafening report had done to my ears.

Jack said something. I could not hear him, but from the way his mouth moved, from the look on his face, he was saying something about justice, or maybe vengeance.

Then he stopped, his face thoughtful, intent.

He was staring down at the corpse.

Perhaps he realized at the last minute what was really happening. The body refused to evaporate. It stayed real. It stayed inevitable.

He squinted in disbelief, staring even more intently. He started trembling then, and not from the cold.

Jack, now the only Jack here, turned toward me. His eyes were haunted. "You said I went to some sort of trouble, more than I remembered, to set this up. But all I did was go to your office. Luciano recommended you. We talked about killing a man. What did you mean? What don't I remember?"

"A lot, Mr. K. For starters, you don't remember who punched you in the eye. You don't remember entering my office, or what we talked about for the first twenty minutes. You don't remember what you had in your hands. The bowling bag, with a helmet inside.

"We talked about killing a man," I continued. "That part you remember. But you don't remember how many times I told you not to do it. You should have listened. It's too late now."

Maybe Jack was listening, or maybe not. He was staring in horror at his gun hand. Mist was trickling up from between his fingers. Of course that was where the paradox would spread out from. That was the epicenter.

He dropped Aaron Burr's pistol clattering to the bloodstained floor and screamed, grabbing his left hand with his right. Now the flesh was boiling off his hand, turning into white and ghostly smoke, and the ghosts of his fingers, in every possible position his hand might have been in or could be in, surrounded the stump of his disintegrating arm like the branches of a swaying tree. The flesh of his face was already transparent when he screamed, and his eyes, rimmed with red muscles, were staring out, horror-stricken, from his bone-white skull. His other arm and his leg was also fading into mist, and the mists were rapidly dissipating.

The sound of his pleading was the worst. It was not just his voice, begging me to save him, begging the girl, begging the dead guy, begging the Masters of Time, because a multitude of his voices were speaking all at once, saying all the possible things he might have said at this point, overlapping, interrupting.

I understand temporal paradox is a painful way to go, since the nervous system, as it disintegrates, sends contradictory signals from all your dispersing versions into the pain center of your brain. He seemed like a brave man. I am sure at least some versions did not complain or beg, or maybe one version said a prayer, or something. But it was lost in the throng.

Getting paradoxed to death is not pretty.

Then he was gone, and the silence after the final shrieks was so silent it seemed like ringing in my ears. The girl had fallen quiet. She sat there on the bed with her hand over her mouth, struck dumb by the terrible sights and sounds.

The old man was silent too, lying dead in a puddle of gore on the floor. I stepped over to him, reached down, put my foot on the walking stick, and yanked off the gold knob. Examining it, I could see the markings around the equator. The top hemisphere could turn independently of the bottom, like a dial.

My foot went numb, which was not pleasant. There was a stunner built into the shaft of the walking stick. Why was it still on? Then I saw that the old man had been using it to numb the pain of being kicked when he was down. So he would die and not suffer. I did not see how to turn the damned thing off, so I drew my gun and set the stick on fire.

I turned to the girl. "Helen!" I tossed the golden knob doohickey toward her. No, I was not trying to make her drop the silk bedsheet draping her nubile form when she raised her hands to catch the watch.

She tore her eyes from the place in midair where Jack was no longer standing, and, now, never had been, and caught it instinctively. She must have had at least partly hardened memory, because she seemed to remember the scene, but the memory must have been hard for her to recall. She had that dreamy, confused look a woman just waking from sleep sometimes has.

"That's not my real name," she said. "It's a stage name."

"It'll do."

She held up the golden device. "Pretty. What is it?"

"Consolation prize. You've been through a lot tonight, Missus, uh, Helen."

The silk bedsheet did slip about an inch while she held up the dingus and smiled at it. At a time like this, in the same room where she had been violated by a human bag of filth, I caught myself looking at her, thinking about her, the same way he had done. The same way Queequeg looks at people: as lunchmeat. Something you use for you.

I turned my eyes away, which I probably should have done from the get-go. She was not dressed decently, and I was definitely not thinking decently. Does that idea seem old-fashioned? Not in my day, it wasn't. It was just coming into vogue. It was needed. The long party of the Roaring Twenties stopped roaring, choked up and sputtered into a world without work, with war in the air, with polio stalking the land. The good old days.

So I missed the beginning of what she was saying.

"...And it's Miss. He didn't marry me. I mean– I *was* a Missus. I've been married. A lot. Jim and Joe and Arthur, and then the Time Travelers came and got me, and then there was the problem with Menelaus and Paris. Theseus didn't count. Jack. And his brother, Bob. They don't count either." She sighed. "Somehow it just never works out."

I nodded. "You might find that gizmo in your hand useful. It's for when you start to get wrinkles and gray hair. If you want to stay young and pretty, twist the dial counterclockwise to get younger. It adjusts the time tensions in your body, but you won't move through time, and your mind stays the same. It's only got a nine-inch range, though. You got to keep it on you, in your purse or your pocket."

She could use it and I couldn't. Guys in my line of work never get old enough to turn gray. I looked down at the almost-headless body, still as real and solid and inevitable as a hangover after a wild bender. Nature always takes revenge when you give in, doesn't she? But sometimes you can help her along.

The hands which lay limp and lifeless on the floor were no longer thin and blue with protruding arteries, dark with liver spots. They were healthy and suntanned and strong.

"Hey, Mister."

"What is it, doll?" I looked at her.

"So, do I have to hire you to solve the mystery?" She pointed to Jack's dead, but younger hands. I caught myself staring at her again, and turned my eyes back toward the corpse.

"What mystery is that?" I said a little gruffly.

"What happened to the third guy? Why did he look young then old? Didn't the wrong body vanish? This time travel makes my head hurt."

The girl was brighter than she looked. She must have guessed at least part of what had happened here. I did not want to tell her the whole story. It would give her nightmares.

I picked up Aaron Burr's pistol. I could feel the tingle of time-energy flowing through it. It was a museum piece from a famous duel. Some Time Warden had long ago made immune it to category-two paradoxes. That was why the pistol did not disappear even though everything else Jack had brought into the scene, his tie and jacket and coat and shoes, all vanished when he erased himself. And every shot the pistol fired still had been fired, even if in this version there was no cause-and-effect explanation for who shot whom or how the gun had gotten there in the first place.

"Time Travel makes everyone's head hurt," I grumbled. "It should be against the law. Makes people think they can get away with anything. Steal anything. Steal women. Use men. Treat everyone else like toys and trophies and furniture, like fashion accessories."

She said, "I know what that is like. It happens when you are famous. You cannot count on people."

"How's that?" I did not see what she was getting at.

She sighed again, and for the first time I really looked at her face, and saw a sad and confused young woman caught up in something she did not understand any more than I understand the deeper mysteries of time travel.

"People use you," she said, "When you are famous. Fame will go by, and, so long, I've had you, fame. If it goes by, I've always known it was fickle. So at least it's something I experienced, but that's not where I live."

"How do you stand it?" I said softly. "People—men like that—"

She shrugged, and now she was wearing her professional face again, a smiling and empty-headed mask she held like a bleached-blonde shield between her and a hungry world. "What can you do? Scream? It only flips their switch, some of them. Fight? They only hit you harder, and if you are bruised you can't work the next day. Kill yourself? I've done it. Sleeping pills are painless, you know? It's just like falling into a fuzzy dark cloud, all warm and floaty. But then I wake up again. The Masters of Time wake me up. Because I'm famous, see? You can't get away from it, not here."

It was a very sad smile.

If I had been any kind of man, I would have knelt down there, and then, like a knight from the Medieval Level of the Frankish tower, sworn to protect her with my life. I did not think she was acting, not just then. The girl truly needed help.

Instead I knelt, picked up a corner of the bloody carpet, and heaved, and managed to throw a large triangular fold of the carpet over the face of the dead man. The inevitable dead man.

"So what happened, Mister?" said the girl, wiping her gorgeous eyes and sniffing. "What really happened?"

"Your boyfriend killed an old man who molested you. Justice was served. Happy ending."

She played with the knob in her hand, and suddenly looked five years younger, mid-twenties rather than mid-thirties. Right at the peak of her glamour. Made my eyes almost hurt to look at her.

She said, "Is this a happy ending? How come neither of us feel happy?"

"I dunno," I was looking around to see where I had put my hat, so I could put it on and leave. Then I remembered it had gone flying over the side of the bridge. "All this just for two cartons of cigarettes. They better be there when I get back to my place."

She grinned briefly, then looked shy and hugged the sheet closer to her as if she were outside, cold and alone. The sinuous folds of the silk clung to her body and emphasized her curves. "I can't stay here. I've got no place of my own. Can I… stay with you?"

Sure, I could take her back to my place. She needed help. She was scared. She was lovely. And she was still inching the knob down, creeping closer to an age that is not legal in some jurisdictions. She was just a kid.

At first I would tell her to sleep on the floor, or maybe I would be the gentleman and take the floor and give her the couch. And then the next morning, I would tell her she had to be gone by that evening, and the next morning after that I would tell her the same thing and so on for a week until it became a joke between us. She would gaze into my eyes and smile and maybe kiss me on the nose and pour me a cup of coffee whenever I said it.

And then, perhaps, when I was old, I would think back upon those days, and I would scour the city looking for an active crystal with the right time depth so I could go back and see her. And then…

And then I would find myself in the same position as the man I'd just helped to kill. Hell, in this damned City, I might end up literally becoming him. I know how time travel works. It lures you in. It seduces you.

It wasn't too hard to step over the corpse and turn my back on her. The smell of the corpse helped.

"You can stay with my pal, Homer. He likes doughnuts and he'll like asking you questions about how the war in Troy turned out."

"It was bad. Everybody died," she said, pouting and nibbling her lip. "Astyanax, they threw him from the roof. He was just a little boy. Then they burned the whole place down. Like I said, somehow it just never works out."

*And Homer is blind, so maybe he can stand to be around you and survive.* I did not say that part out loud, only to myself.

Look, I don't blame the dame for using the tools Nature gave her any more than I blame a spider. But I'd seen one guy trapped in her web, and I'd heard all about the others. Even if it was a web she did not spin on purpose, she was a spider. Guys like Paris, guys like the Yankee Clipper, even guys like Jack lost their hearts over this girl, lost their minds, lost their good names. Sometimes they even lost their lives.

I don't think she did anything on purpose, but maybe she was part of the cold justice in this cold world, the justice that took its revenge on the men who used her and hurt her.

I waited outside while she was getting dressed, glad that without my hat it was so cold. It kept me from thinking bad thoughts.

She chatted with me as we walked, me stomping and her swaying and bouncing, and slipped her hand very naturally through my elbow and clutched my arm, sending something like an electric shock up my spine, from groin to brain. I remember the way she smelled, the way she tucked a stray curl into her little Santa Claus hat with a delicate motion of her hand. I've never been that close to anyone so damned pretty in my life.

She looked so lost, so woebegone, and yet so cheerful when she smiled, that I admired her inner strength, even as I grieved for the kind of life she was trapped in.

I was glad at that moment I had done what I did, glad I had watched a man die in utmost pain as he dissolved into mist. I had helped with the world's cold justice. You see, hers was the face that was innocent and bewildered at the cruel hurts done to her. Hers was a face without hope. Without hope, yet with a bright smile. Without hope, yet soldiering on.

But how can you have hope in this city? Hope comes when you have an unknown future waiting like a Christmas gift, shining in its pink-bowed wrapping paper, and every tomorrow is a new surprise to open.

Hope is when you can change your future. But if the Time Wardens can step through a crystal into your tomorrow, and they can change your tomorrow, but you cannot, then all the gifts have already been opened and all the toys are theirs.

When we got there, she said: "Thanks for everything!" and stood up on her tiptoes to kiss my cheek. But I drew back and put my hand up before those lips, those lips I had been surreptitiously staring at, and wondering about, could land.

Maybe you remember the Kit Marlowe's line: 'Sweet Helen, make me immortal with a kiss. But do you know the next one? I looked it up. 'Her lips suck forth my soul: see where it flies!'

You think maybe there is a version of the scene where she planted that kiss and my soul was sucked out, and I grabbed her and bent her over my arm and canoodled her something awful. And maybe the part she plays and hides behind would have kissed me back, but it would have killed the little girl inside. But I got hardened memory. I know there is no other version.

"No charge, this time, Ma'am." I said. If they give out awards for the most awkward line any man ever said, keep that one in mind.

"It's still Miss," she said, smiling. "You know. *Miss.* Because things never quite work out. I keep trying to hit a life. A normal life. I keep missing. Guess that is where that word comes from."

Her red mitten seemed very small and soft in my black glove. She did not shake hands, but merely put her fingertips in my palm, like girls from my day used to do.

I did not want to let her go, not right away. So I said: "You don't like being Helen of Troy? All the famous poets sing about you, Miss."

"Fame is wonderful," she said, with her cat-ate-the-canary smile, her eyes half-closed, speaking in that breathy way she had, as she turned from me and spoke over her shoulder, "But you can't curl up with it on a cold night."

I left her with Homer and I went home, and my arm, without a girl on it, without the girl on it, felt cold.

I found the two cartons of cigarettes, as promised.

So I sat in the dark, smoking, a point of fire held at my fingertips, letting the dark scent of the tobacco drive away the last traces of her lingering perfume.

At least it was a happy ending for me.


## SECOND INTERMISSION

There is one detail I don't want to forget to tell you.

Earlier, back on day three thousand twenty-eight, back in my office, watching Edward Teach give me a nasty smile over his shoulder as he swaggered away after his boss, I realized that what was bothering me was not the man's outrageous beard, which practically reached to his eyebrows. I was bothered by a continuity error in Jack's story, at least the part I had heard.

I looked over at where the helmet still sat on the floor next to the couch, where he had let it slip through his dazed fingers as the effect took hold. I still did not want to touch the damned thing. But now I wished I had asked him one question I could no longer ask. What had happened from his point of view? The point of view that was just erased?

Jack's memory was fairly hard, and so, to him, getting shot and then suddenly finding himself in the scene that never happened was no different from me getting killed and having the circuit in my gun retroactively erect a nimbus a moment in the past, and suddenly being never-killed half a hiccup in the direction of elsewhen.

The helmet probably just erased the hardened parts of the memories, the anachronisms. It should be easy, given Time Warden technology, to turn into mist those memories in your head that, from the point of view of the time continuum, came from nowhere for no reason.

But from the point of view of the non-dead Jack, his personal continuity, what happened? I assume the shooter and his gun disappeared into mist before the trigger was pulled. Which meant that the job he had hired me to do could not get done.

Well, Hell. I was not going to let that happen, not if I could help it. I needed to find a gun that would not vanish into the discontinuity mists.

A few minutes later, with the bowling bag and the accursed helmet under my arm, I found a newsboy at the corner of two bridges willing to swap me a paper for a half-empty carton of melted strawberry ice cream. He agreed. Some people are just desperate, I guess.

Ben Franklin and William Howard Russell published the paper. Beneath words of wisdom from Poor Richard, was the Recurring Events section. There I found the announcement of the next duel between Aaron Burr and Alexander Hamilton.

I may have a hard life, but I am glad I am not Aaron Burr. Imagine having a hardened memory, and remembering Hamilton's pistol ball pass through various parts of your body, breaking bones and piercing organs of which you are particularly fond, rolling in agony on the ground in a pool of your own blood, leaving you maimed or leaving you dying, slowly or quickly, over and over again, and knowing it would happen again tomorrow, as part of the opening ceremonies at the beginning of every horserace between the Blue and Green. And all because some Time Warden thinks it is funny that Alex Hamilton is a much better shot than you.

I patted the bowling bag tucked under my arm. I guessed Old Aaron would be delighted to swap, and I wanted to get rid of this thing. Probably as bad as he wanted to get rid of the memories of his endless duel with Hamilton.

Why couldn't they just forgive and forget? Can't people change?

## THE MIDDLE

The second time I met Jack, it was in my office. This was on day three thousand twenty-eight, about noon.

He was sitting on my couch. It is a pretty nice couch, actually, because I don't have a bed, and I sleep on it. The gold helmet was sitting on the floor next to the arm of the couch, right where it had been dropped.

I was not going to pick it up. I did not want to touch it.

You can understand why such an instrument would be useful in a city full of retired time travelers, people who like to play God with other people's pasts and futures. No matter how unlikely it was that someone would develop the theory and practice of such a hideous machine, rest assured, the Time Wardens were bound to fiddle with the timelines until they produced a version of history that led to a helmet like this.

Jack groaned as if he was having a bad dream. Little did he know that any nightmare was better than what was he was about wake up into.

He sat up suddenly, like a punch-drunk fighter hearing the bell. "What– what just happened?"

"You took a nap on the couch." Which was true as far as it went.

He rubbed his eyes, got up, frowning in puzzlement. He touched his black eye and he winced.

"Quite a shiner you got there," I said. "You box? You been in a fight?"

He looked around my office for a moment, touching the tender black flesh around his swollen eye. "No, I don't remember—who hit me? Who let me get hurt?"

Who let me get hurt? That said something about his character. Not something good.

"You left your men outside," I said. "Step out the door, take a look. Ask them the time and date, if you think you've been time-ducted.

Ask them what you are doing here."

Jack raised his voice. "Eddy!"

My outer door opened instantly, as if the guy had been keeping his hand on the knob. Blackbeard the Pirate stuck his shaggy head in. He had his sword and flintlock stuck through his sash, and firecrackers tied to his beard (which covered his cheeks almost to his nose) and fuses under his hat, but nothing was drawn and the freakish beard was not lit. Thank goodness.

"Yes, Mr. President? Is ought nae proper, sir?"

"Tell me the date, and where we came from, Mr. Teach."

Blackbeard was not surprised at the question. He'd been in Metachronopolis long enough to know the ropes. "Sixty-three days since your last, sir. You done burned the ken at the grogshop with Lucky Luciano, and crossed here with me and me boys through the Japanner Tower. I reckon but an hour past, sir."

*Burned the ken*, in case your doohickey that retroactively feeds Eighteenth Century slang into your head goes haywire, is when strollers leave an alehouse without paying their quarters. I reminded myself to get paid in advance.

"Why am I here?" Jack said.

Blackbeard looked at me narrowly. He said, "To silent a man after pommeling him right, sir. Some rum cull snabbled your frisky game-pullet. You came here to dawb Jakes the Miller."

That would be yours truly. Jacob is my Christian name. Miller is slang for a murderer, a killer.

"How did I get this black eye?" asked Jack. "Did someone hit me?"

Blackbeard looked astounded, at least, as astounded as a man can look when you can only see a T-shape of flesh surrounding his beady eyes and big beak of a nose. "How would I be knowing if you're nae telling?"

"When did it happen?"

"Yesterday. On sixty-two. Out you went alone on privy business, abram of your loyal bullies. You come back with that knock on your costard. Never cackled who fetched you that culp."

Jack waved him away and Blackbeard closed the door. I took out my gizmo that deadens any outgoing noise, and set the zone to exclude everything outside the door. If business were better, I would have a waiting room out there, but it is just a section of hall where I put some chairs and a desk for Penny.

Jack said apologetically. "Mr. Teach does not know what a private detective is. He thinks you are an assassin. I only want you to find a certain man."

"All right. And then?"

"Then assassinate him."

I shook my head. "I am telling you not to do it. It is suicidal. I mean that literally. You won't survive the scene."

Jack crossed over to the chair in front of my desk and sat down. He put his elbows on the desk, but he was a client, so I said nothing.

He said, "I remember walking in the door. Lucky recommended you. He says you always keep your word. He told me, there was this time you had been hired by the one gang to guard a shipment of opium due in from the Second Century, but another gang hired you to leave the side door of the cargo carrier unlocked."

"Blues and Greens," I said. "The horse-racing factions. The game was crooked in their day too, back in Byzantium. They were political factions, too, and they played for keeps back then."

The Wardens swept up some of them from out of the time stream, and looked at them and played with them and asked them questions, but no one is sent home again from Metachronopolis, and the Wardens don't really much care what you do once they're done with you. The Blues sided with Richelieu and the Capone gang, and the Greens took up with Hannibal and Billy the Kid's outfit, and their ancient, meaningless fight continues.

He said, "You left the door open, as promised, and when the Green's men started to come in, you took a meat cleaver in one hand and a switchblade in the other and killed the whole mob of them. So you protected the shipment, also as promised."

"Don't believe everything you hear. It was a khopesh, not a meat cleaver. There were only three guys, and I only maimed them."

"You kept your word."

"Technically, yes," I said. "If I take the case, the man you are hunting down will die. The culprit will come to justice. But I won't kill him. And you won't survive."

"You cannot know that for sure," he said.

"It's a done deal."

"How can you know?"

"Because I already found the guy. He came back to the now. He wants to see her."

I whistled for the magic picture. Sometimes it works, sometimes it doesn't. This time it did, and the image of Old Glory I have on the wall to the left, right above the dream coffin and next to my broken Anything Maker, shimmered and formed a nice poster of the perpetrator. He was lounging at the side of a pool on some high level of a Tower near the Museum of Man, which loomed in the background, a stepped pyramid larger than Everest, rising from a misty base. The pool was one of those fancy types from the Mid Twenty-Ninth Century, two lenticular shapes of water, one above the other held in midair by some sort of manipulation of Van Der Waals repulsion. A swimmer could swim out of the bottom of the upper pool and swan-dive through the air into the lower. The special properties of the water also allowed bathing beauties wearing Saint Peter Slippers to stand upright on the water surface, which bent under their weight like a rubbery sheet of clear gelatin.

That was what six beauties were doing now. It was a beauty contest, between five versions of Helen of Troy and her ancient rival Cleopatra. Don Juan was one of the judges, and so was Jacques Casanova de Seingalt. Seated right behind them, in the top-hat-and-white-tie VIP section, was our perpetrator. He was leaning on a gold-headed cane.

"It's you," I said. "You're the criminal you want to kill. The man you want to protect the girl from is you."

His eyes narrowed slightly. That was all.

"You are not surprised." I observed dryly.

"I wish I were. I– I may not be that kind of man. Not now. But my father– ah, well, never mind." He squinted. "I thought he would be older."

"Older you is about thirty years prophet of you now. He's in his late seventies, early eighties. When he holds that walking stick—see the cane with the gold knob?—he looks as young as he wants. He can look your age. Or forty, or thirty. It's also got a stunner built into it so no one can take it from him."

"How can he look so young?"

"Magic."

"Really?"

I shrugged. "The Wardens can adjust the time energy tension in your body without influencing your thoughts or memories, but, heck, just call it magic. I'm not paid to understand things, just to hunt men and break heads."

"And if I pay you to–"

"Then you'll die."

He shook his head. "Not necessarily!"

"In this case, necessarily. Look, pal, I been around the block. Back in your world, you were the boss. You understood things. Here, you are a greenhorn, wet behind the ears. How long you been here?"

"Not long. But I think I understand how time travel works. If I go to her room when he is there, my older self, and I shoot him dead, then me, the I that I am now, all I have to do is look down at my own corpse at my feet and know that this is my sure and certain fate. I'll know I can never go to her again. I can decide and stick with the decision. The moment I make that decision, the future is changed. They say the body lying on the ground will turn into what they call a mist, an overlap of many possible futures, and then fade entirely. Turn into smoke. That's what happens, right?"

"That is what happens if a ghost, a man's self from his own past, shoots his prophet, a self from his own future. Some ghosts, seeing the prophesied future, can change their minds and change it hard enough that the inevitable turns evitable, and the chances change. So the certain future gets uncertain, changes its mind, and evaporates into mist. But—"

"But what? Surely you don't think I lack the strength of character, the willpower, to—I mean, if I saw my own death, as clear and certain as doomsday itself—if the choice were between the future as a man who gets executed by his own hand on a certain date, and a long life here in Metachronopolis!"

I said, "No one listens to the prophets. They stone them instead."

"But if I saw my own future, caused my own future? You think I could do that and see that and still not change? If it were a matter life and death?"

"Some men prefer death, sir," I said, leaning back in my chair and letting my eyes look at the ceiling. I did not want to look at his face. "Even self-inflicted. They find it's the only way to sooth a raw conscience."

"What are you saying? What are you implying?"

I brought my eyes down and locked gazes with him, and my chair fell forward so the front legs hit the floor with a bang. "Prove it. Right now. Right here. You say you can change your future, fine, then let's see you change yourself, give up the girl, and never see her again."

I pointed at the magic picture. The sound came on. Cleopatra was just finishing a song from one of her shows and then said something about world peace. Now it was Helen of Troy's turn.

She was doing a number about diamonds being a better friend to women than men could be. It was catchy.

I pointed at the three other Helens in the view. "Helen of Troy is a popular girl. The most popular, you might say. Which one is yours?"

"What? They all look the same."

"You've been in bed with this girl. Held her in your arms. Do you talk to her? You cannot tell the difference? Their hairstyles are not the same. They wear different ear rings. You don't know what her bathing suit looks like? These are the details a man would know about his wife. If he loved her. If he lived with her."

He looked at his shoe, at my pen blotter, at the door, at the dream box, at everything but my eyes. "I have other, ah, responsibilities, Mr. Frontino. The Time Wardens have put me in charge of one of their projects related to my era, investigations of conspiracy theories throughout history. People are depending on me to—and, well, there's Jackie—my people don't believe in divorce, so—"

I whistled for the magic picture again, and focused the view on the man seated behind Don Juan and Casanova. All three men wore the same expression, by the way.

"There he is," I said, pulling up the pen on my desk Jack was looking at, and throwing it across the room like a dart. The pen point bounced off the image of Old Jack. Right between the eyes. I wished I had thrown it hard enough to stick right in the middle of the magic picture, and make that satisfying thump and quiver of a bullseye shot. Young Jack was startled, turned his head as the pen flew whistled past his ear, so he was looking straight into the eyes of old Jack.

"So there he is, pal," I said, drawling my words slowly. "Vow him out of existence."

"What?"

"All you got to do is vow never to see the girl again, never get close to her. If you don't see her, you can't put your hands on her, can't do anything illegal, can't get violent, can't make any more whoopee. If you can do it, do it now. Mend your character. Be a man. Make that future vanish."

Jack stood up, a determined look on his face, and turned toward the image.

I looked at my fingernails, noticed they were grimy, got out my switchblade, flicked it open, and picked the grit out from under my nails one at a time. I worked slowly and carefully so as not to cut myself, first the left hand, and, not so easily, the right. All the while I hummed a tuneless tune.

Then I put the knife away and stood up. Jack was still there. So was the image in the magic picture. No mist, no change. Jack was wiping his eyes, as if he had suffered some tremendous strain, staring into the sun, or into his own grave, or maybe he was weeping.

He said in a ragged voice. "It will be different if I am actually looking down at the body. My own body. Killed by me. If I look down, and the body turns to mist, I will know I can change my fate. If I know that if I give in, it will mean death, certain death, if I knew it, then I could be...I could be—"

"Be strong?" I suggested.

"Be normal."

I stood up, picked up my hat, tossed it in the air, caught it, placed it on my head at a jaunty angle. "All right. I'll take the case. I'll help you kill yourself. You deserve it."

He wiped his eyes and glared at me. "You have a big mouth for a hired gun."

"Do I, boss? Tell me how you met this girl again? Your Helen of Troy? Ah, no answer, eh? Well, I'll let that pass. And you'll have to leave your bully boys behind when we go in tomorrow night. I am going to do just what I said I would do, just like last time. Protect the girl from the man who attacked her."

"What do you mean, 'last time'?"

"Never mind that. Remember the price we agreed on?

"Two cartons of cigarettes? Is that all a human life is worth to you?"

I shrugged. "I take people as they come."

"How do you sleep at night, Mr. Frontino?"

I pulled out my shoulder holster, shrugged my arms into it, and then walked over to the hatrack for my coat. "I like to smoke before I sleep. Helps me relax. So our deal will work out nicely. Happy ending. You shoo your boys away. I got to lock up. Meet you downstairs, and then you take me to see your girl so we can go over some instructions and set up our little trap for tomorrow night."

"What do you mean? You think—as soon as tomorrow?"

I looked at the Magic Picture. Sitting behind Don Juan and old Jack was what looked like a headless suit of armor wearing trenchcoat and a slouch hat. With a Frankish axe at one shoulder. A Tin Woodman.

Some sort of mechanical man with no head. So that is what my visitor from yesterday meant.

At that moment, a line of scantily clad girls danced in a bouncing fashion across the bouncing surface of the water, all kicking in unison, laughing and singing.

"He is thirty years in his own past," I said. "The beauty contest must have been an event whose date he found a way to look up, even in this city where no one has a calendar. I can see why folk remembered it. But he is not a Time Warden, so if he is here, he is not here for long. Maybe he has been here all week, or, more likely, he was given a destiny crystal by a Warden to give him two anchor points, one tomorrow, when the beauty contest festivities end, and one seven days ago. Tonight she has her talent show competition, and he'll certainly go see that. He'll strike tomorrow. I mean, look at those dames! You know what he feels when he sees her. Now imagine not being able to see her for thirty years. Look at that look on your face."

While he was staring at his older version, I whistled at the magic picture and turned it into a looking glass. Jack saw himself wearing much the same hungry expression as the old man, and he looked ashamed.

Then he turned and marched toward the door, shouting for Blackbeard and his men.

Edward Teach opened the door and held it open politely. Behind Jack's back, Teach met my eye, and gave me an ugly smile of camaraderie. By some unspoken clue, Teach knew I had been hired, and so now I was like him, just more hired muscle, just another cutthroat, and that made his yellow teeth appear in the wild thicket of his pyromaniacal beard. It is the kind of smile the Madame at the cathouse gives to a preacher man when he shows up as a customer.

My conscience was squawking at me like a dim and tinny voice over the wireless under bad atmospheric conditions, telling me what that grin meant, but I had years of practice in not letting myself figure out what I did not want to know. You see, I am smart that way.

## THE BEGINNING

The first time I met Jack was the day before, day three thousand and twenty-seven since my being hired (or being abducted, not that is there any difference) by the Masters of Metachronopolis, also called the Time Wardens. I was sitting in the middle of the floor of my office, playing mumbly-peg with the switchblade I'd been given as a reward and a memento for tracking down the Serb. I had a two-pound cardboard carton of ice cream that I had given up trying to finish.

He flung open the door and stood in the doorway. We looked at each other with some surprise.

"Who the Hell are you?" I growled. Normally, I try to say heck, but not when people break in.

"Your secretary is out," he said.

"I got no secretary. Penny is the ice cream man's daughter. She pretends she's my receptionist when I have an appointment with some chump. Looks more professional that way. Now who, I repeat, the Hell are you, barging in here without knocking? Also, do you want some ice cream? I can't eat it all before it melts and the carton is leaking. And I hate strawberry."

"Why are you eating it, then?"

"This is my breakfast, lunch and dinner. The icebox is empty and the Anything Maker is broke. And I was hungry. So, who are you? This is last time I'll ask without a gun or a knife or baseball bat and painful but undetectable soft tissue damage being involved in some capacity."

"I am a chump."

"What?"

"Your chump. One of your clients. You work for me. Or you will this time tomorrow."

I sighed. "Is this one of those cases where you hire me to solve a murder, and you end up being the murderer yourself? Or the victim? Or both?"

He looked embarrassed. "Well, to be quite honest—"

I stood up. "That would be a yes. Which means a no. I don't take cases from Time Wardens."

"I am not a Warden. Not yet. But I have prestige."

"Enough to time travel just a bit? Just a wee bit?"

"That's right," he nodded.

"Like being a wee bit pregnant. You can time travel a wee bit at first, but sooner or later you'll end up eating yourself like a snake who swallows his own tail and is not bright enough to know when to stop chewing. Go away. You can commit anachronistic multiple-suicide by yourself without my help."

"Does that happen a lot?"

"You'd be surprised."

"I can pay. Two cartons of cigarettes."

I circled the desk, and sat down in the chair with a sigh, wiped the ice cream off my fingers, straightened my tie, and ran my fingers through my hair. Now I looked like a professional. "In that case, welcome. Please take a seat, Mr., ah?"

"Kennedy. But you can call me Jack."

If I had been a dog, my ears would have stood straight up and quivered. "Jack 'Quail Hunter' Kennedy, outlaw and train robber? You were shot to death by half-a-dozen railroad agents and postal inspectors! You were the last! The last great train robber of the Old West!"

"No, that's not me. I'm the President of the United States."

"President? Well, I guess you won't get shot to death, then. Glad to hear the United States is still around in the future. Now why are you trying to kill yourself and why the hell should I give a damn?"

He pulled out an envelope, passed it to me. "Here are my references. Recognize the handwriting? This is a letter from you to you."

He sat quietly while I read the letter.

I looked up. "When did I write this?"

"After I shot myself. My older version shot my oldest version. He—the oldest one—just lay there on the floor, and he didn't– he didn't disappear. That means I can't—it means I won't be able—to stop myself. When the time comes. Even though I know I am going to die, I will still walk into it. Walk into it with eyes open!"

I nodded. Time travelers never enter a scene unless they are satisfied with the outcome. "So, then," I said, "From what it says here, you're not happy with the outcome of shooting yourself, so therefore you are going to hire me tomorrow to go shoot your prophet-self. Walk into it with eyes open, so to speak. Do I detect a modicum of irony here?"

He shook his head. "It's not that simple."

"It never is."

"And there is this girl."

"There always is." I shrugged. "So how did you get back here and what do you want from me? You're a double-dipper? I mean you came from your own future into your personal past?"

"Yes. No. I mean I did come back, or I will, but I'm not the me who did. I just talked to him. To me."

"Start from the beginning."

"A time traveler came to me. He wore a hood and I could not see his face. I sent my men away, and he shows me that he is me, myself from the future. He tells me this story, of the version of me from tomorrow, my tomorrow, hiring you to help me kill the older me. He said the story does not have a happy ending."

"Stories involving time travel never do."

"He said after he killed the old man, and he did not dissolve, he realized that retaliation was not enough. I would still turn into him, despite seeing the future with my own eyes. The self-murder did not fix anything. It was empty. The version of me in the future is still committing the crime, and the version of Norma Jean who exists now was still... attacked last week. I don't want revenge. I want to change the past. To stop the rape from ever happening."

I said, "Put a pistol in your mouth and pull the trigger. Bang. Old you is gone. No future."

He shook his head. "Suicide is a sin."

I blinked at that. People are odd. "So is cheating on your wife," I said blandly. "And hiring a hit man. Not to mention a few other things I could name."

He said, "I won't pull the trigger on myself. I just won't."

"But stepping in front of another version of you who you know will kill you, that's okay? It's the same as stepping in front of a speeding locomotive. And it is still you killing you."

"It's different. Future me is not me now."

"So it's not you, you don't give a damn? Never mind that. I don't need the excuses, just the facts. So how did you get back here?"

"I didn't. I am the version from here and now. I just have not come to see you at your office yet."

I blinked again. Hate this city. I can never keep track of who is which and when is now. "Start from the beginning again. And this time, from the beginning beginning."

"It's easier if I start at the end and work backwards."

"I usually do it that way myself," I admitted. "Go ahead. How does the story end?"

"The oldest version of me is the bad one. The attacker. The tomorrow version of me, you might say the middle one, comes to see you, hires you, and the next day the two of you go to stop the oldest version of me in the room where I keep Norma Jean. Middle me shoots the old me, but old me does not turn into mist. That means the rape still will happen, and that I will still turn into him. Turn into the evil old bastard. Even seeing my own dead body was not enough! So what is enough? There was a shower stall in the suite, and it was actually a door through time. It is set to three points. One is thirty years from now, where old me-to-be is squire to the Time Wardens, and is set to be elevated to be a Warden. Soon. The second anchor point is set the day after tomorrow, in the evening, when old me comes to repeat his crime. Tomorrow is when middle me, vendetta-me, comes and hires you to exact revenge on old me. You go with him, but he pulls the trigger. But then the body does not disappear, as he expected. He asked you for help. You wrote that letter, and sent him into the hidden destiny glass in the shower, so he goes ahead thirty years, where he is a Time Warden, and has access to all their machinery, all their powers. Are you following this?"

I nodded. "I've had practice. Around here you hear a lot of stories like this. So what happens next? Middle Jack finds you five days ago, the Young Jack, and explains what is about to happen?"

He smiled his charming smile. "No. The time traveler who came to me is not from our timeline at all. He is the me I should have been, the one who never committed any crimes in the first place, any of them. The better version of me. An innocent Jack. The one I want to make real."

That struck me as suspicious. "I've never heard of anything like that."

"That does not mean it is not true. Listen. Innocent Jack told me the plan. There is a moment in time where old me is not protected by this body guard thing, some sort of mechanical man with no head. You ran out of the door with me, and the bodyguard followed us, trying to stay in the way between you and me."

"Makes sense. Old Jack has to protect Middle Jack from being killed, or else Old Jack gets erased."

"This guard, whatever it is, Innocent Jack told me said it had a five-minute time range. If it is kept away from old me for five minutes, then there is the time where old me can be killed. Oh, and this is the important point: you have to shoot the bathroom!"

"What? Why do I have to shoot the bathroom?"

"Because I told you to."

"When?"

"No, I mean I am telling you now. This me version of me is telling the you version of now-you to shoot the door. Now. This is me telling you. I am telling you because the innocent parallel version of me told me to, and the older version of you told the middle me to tell other me to tell now-me to tell now-you."

I rubbed my temples. "I don't even like talking to time travelers."

"Because of conversations like this?"

"No. Because conversations like this start to make sense."

"So are you following the sequence of events?" he asked.

I nodded. "Except for how middle-you got to talk to other-you, who you say is innocent, even though he is telling you how to commit a suicide-murder. And what happens to him? Middle-you him, I mean?"

He said, "He appears in the room when you shoot the shower stall door in the bathroom. You did not do it last time, in the first run-through version of the scene, because middle me uses the unbroken door sometime after the shooting to travel into the future and makes contact with other-me, who came back and gave me your letter."

I said, "So the destruction of the door forms an endpoint, which pushes anyone passing down that particular artificial spacetime continuum path back into the real timespace. It is a way of forming an anchor point where there is not supposed to be one. I shoot the door to force a time traveler back into timespace in that bathroom, at the point in time a few seconds before the door fails. And apparently that's you—namely, late middle you."

"No, that is going to be me, me. This version of me. I have a destiny card attuned to the shower stall door that other me got from middle me in the future. The youngest possible Jack has to be the one in the room. When I die, it has to wipe out everyone after me in the timestream."

"You lost me. How did he fool the people thirty years from now? Middle you, I mean. How did he explain that he was fifty instead of eighty?"

"Old me has a walking stick with an age-adjuster built in. Middle me took it, and turned himself into an old man. Then he realized that the old man turned himself into a young man to be strong enough to, ah, do the, ah—"

"Do the girl?"

"I was going to say do the deed. The cane also has a stunner in it that numbs you if it touches a hand, or puts you into a delta wave sleep if it touches your head. Do you know what that is? Magic sleep. I am going to step out of the bathroom once you and early middle me leave the scene, then use it to stun Norma Jean so that she does not wonder why there are two of us in the room. The plan is that I beat old me to death with it, don his medical cape, twist the knob once to turn him into thousand-year-old dust, and twist the knob again to make me look like him... you see?"

"Um... I think I lost track of the order of events."

"A version of me comes by tomorrow to hire you. You take the case and make sure to shoot the bathroom door to form the anchor point so that I can get into the scene. I kill me and take his cape and his age, and put her gently to sleep so she does not see me. You bring me, the tomorrow version of me, middle me, back into the room. He kills his own past version of himself, me. And you don't interfere. I get erased from the timeline."

"What prevents middle you from remembering this conversation? I mean early middle you, the one who hires me tomorrow. Since that scene is in your personal future. It's tomorrow."

"I have a selective amnesia induction field helmet late middle me stole from one of the palaces of old me. A Forgetting Helmet. I was shown how to use it. Tomorrow when I come to this office again, I will bring it with me."

I frowned. "I think there is a screw loose in this plan somewhere. Aren't you dead at this point tomorrow? You get shot while lying on the floor pretending to be old you?"

"No, the plan is perfect! Tomorrow when I visit you, I will shoo my men out, program the helmet, put it on my own head, and forget everything that came from any visit from later-time versions of me, and I'll forget this conversation. All you have to do is shoot the door and watch me evaporate. Everything will be wrapped up in a nice, neat, Gordian knot."

I sighed, and leaned back, and stared at the dark gold ceiling, running my tongue over the sickly sweet taste of strawberries sticking to my teeth.

"So will you take the case?"

I leaned forward again. "Absolutely not. Look, you are already going to kill yourself, and you have already killed yourself, but the version of you who is in front of me now has not done anything yet! You are the innocent one!"

Young Jack looked stricken, but tried to control his expression. "Actually. Uh…"

"You can't truly want to go through with this! This plan? This stupid, crazy plan? You're wearing a crucifix, and I heard beads rattling in your pockets. Aren't you a good Catholic boy? We have Catholic priests here. A guy named Maximilian Kolbe, we call him Father Max, lives two levels down and just around the corner. And Joan of Arc runs a revival meeting on the roof. Go say confession, or get baptized, or do whatever you guys do. Clean yourself up. Then marry your damned chippy. If you love her. Don't you love her?"

"Did I explain who she was?"

"Sure. Helen of Troy. One of them."

He looked surprised. "She is the most famous actresses of all time! Hollywood actress, I mean."

"Not in my time. Silent or talkie?"

He said, "I thought everyone in Metachronopolis had heard the story. The Time Warden Ceuthonymus drew the film actress Elizabeth Taylor back in time and created an alternate history where she was Cleopatra, the Egyptian queen. It was a joke. So, to top him, the Warden Menoetius drew Marilyn Monroe into a timeline where she was Helen of Troy. And she proved to be a prettier Helen than the original, so other Time Wardens made copies of the time line. Then the Wardens got bored, as they do, and Marilyn was sent to do waitress and hostess jobs, or dime-a-dance gigs. Or worse. After I was drawn in, scooped up by the Warden Iapetus, he gave me one as a spare."

Something very cold and very dark entered my heart then. "Gave?"

"As a reward. She's not really my—not what you would call a sweetheart or demimonde—she did not volunteer, you know."

"Is concubine a better word?" I asked softly. "The Wardens gave her to you as a harem girl. A slave."

"Hey, I treat her right! She doesn't act like she minds very much."

"Then she is a good actress. Sexual knowledge without consent is still rape. Why are you still using this girl? What has she ever done to you? To deserve you?"

He did not say anything, so the silence hung over the room exactly like the thick cloud of smoke from my nonexistent cigarette would have if I had one.

"Never mind," I said, "I know the answer. Have you ever wondered why you were chosen by the Time Wardens to join their ranks?"

It was pretty obvious he had, because he looked like he was being crushed inward, as if his spine were squeezing and pulling all his internal organs inward into a smaller and smaller knot.

I said in a louder voice, "That is why they are giving you their little gifts? They want you to get used to the idea of using time travel to evade your problems rather than solve them."

"I am not evading anything! I'm trying to fix it!"

"No. Time travel makes men lazy. If the sweet, sweet worm were not wriggling on the hook of time travel, the fish of your guilty conscience would not rise to the surface to swallow the bait. If it wasn't an option, you would not try to change the past, you would just make amends now, free her now, beg forgiveness from her now, and now straighten out your life. If you could not travel back in time and erase the moment when you dove into the sewer pond, then you would have to clean yourself up, scrape the sewage off your damned soul one painful day at a time."

I drew a breath, a little surprised at myself at how angry I was. He said nothing, but he lowered his eyes, troubled. It seemed I had said something that struck him right in the middle of his soul. I paused to let it sink in.

"Free the girl," I said. "Or marry her. Instead of taking everything in her life away from her, give her everything in your life you can give her. Clean yourself up!"

Not looking up, he said in a whisper: "I thought of doing that. I've tried. But it won't work. I know I don't have whatever it takes, I don't have the willpower."

That annoyed me. His excuse for his behavior was that it was too hard to be decent? "Well, buddy, there is no one else you can turn to for help. In this life, the big fish eat the little fish, and the Time Wardens are the biggest fish there have ever been."

"You're wrong," he said softly, still looking down at his hands.

"I ain't wrong. Listen! I have a friend who is a cannibal, an actual maneater. He looks at people just as slabs of meat to be consumed. Men are not souls to him, they are things. Things to eat. How are you better than that?"

He straightened his spine and looked me in the eye, "I can set things right."

"How? By more time travel? Time travel is cowardly. It's futile. For one thing, if the girl has an even slightly hardened memory, she'll still remember you and what you did to her."

He gritted his teeth and said, with only the smallest quake in his voice, "Then she will also remember that I am willing to die to set things straight!"

"Says who?" I smiled sourly.

"Says the enemies of the Time Wardens. You see, I tried doing this alone. And I can't."

There was something really odd in his voice when he said those words. I sat up in my chair.

"The Masters of Time cannot have enemies," I said slowly. "They would just go back in history and kill their enemy's father, whoever he is."

"You have seen things go into the mist. Things can come out as well! Men, miracles, messengers! Whole worlds emerge from the mist as they pass from being impossible to being inevitable. That includes the first world holding the original version of this city."

I squinted as if against a strong light. "What kind of baloney is that?"

"You've got it all wrong. The purpose of time travel is to forgive and heal. It is to make our past crimes fade away, into the mist of nothingness. But it has been turned wrong here, corrupted by these so-called Time Wardens. They are rebels, a gang of criminals, who abused the machinery of time travel over which they were given stewardship. They use their powers to indulge in their past crimes and to evade consequences. So this has become a city of lies built on a foundation of nothingness. But if, one by one, each Master of Time, even before he is elevated to the position, turns away from the evils he has done and will do, and sponge them out of the pages of history, then this city of evasion will become a city of salvation!"

I wanted to believe him. The Masters of Time certainly acted like a gang of crooks.

"How could you possibly know this? Where did you hear any of this?"

He leaned forward, his eyes burning. "Because old me is only one version of me. He is going to turn into a Time Warden, and he'll be no different from any of them. Dressed in a mirror, with a crown and no face, and wrapped in a robe of mist. As cruel and remorseless as history itself."

"And the other version, he is the one from the other timeline?"

"Yes. He is the one who sent me to you. They have crowns of gold, and their robes are solid black, as black as midnight, because the past good they have done can never be changed. Their city is green rather than gold, and time travel is only used to punish the penitent among them. They do not rule time."

"Anarchists, eh? They just leave all the flatliners alone, do they?"

"They are not the Masters of Time but of Eternity. There is no beginning to them, nothing that can be edited away. They have followed the tradition of the first Moonshot, expanded into space rather than time, and their version of Luna glitters with cities and cathedrals and tabernacles whose light you can see from Earth. You may have seen that Moon, the Moon in the heavens in the timelines where America did not lose hope. The closer the Emerald Towers come to being real, the less real these proud Towers of accursed gold become, and the clearer and fairer shines the cities of Luna."

"You know—must know—I don't believe you."

He smiled and leaned back. "I don't care if you believe me now or not. I think you will, eventually. The other me, the Master of Eternity who comes from a world of a bright moon above towers of shining green above a fruitful world of green grass and green forest— he told me you were the man."

"What man?"

"The man who sees the downfall of the last of the Masters of Time. I was told to come to you because you are a man who is not afraid. And because—sometimes—you listen to your conscience."

I shook my head. "You were told a fairy tale. It's some sort of Chronocrat trick. If old you is about to become a Time Warden himself, then my guess is some other Wardens, unfriendly Wardens, who, for reasons you will never know, have decided to sweep your seventh-row pawn off the board before it turns into a Queen. I don't know what version of yourself visited you when, but if you were visited by a time traveler, then you can be sure it was a Warden."

"He was an honest and decent man."

"An honest and decent Warden? No such thing. The whole point of giving you the girl, giving you power, tempting and corrupting you, was to make you the kind of man who thinks like a Time Warden. If this anarchist guy who says he is their enemy were real, he would not use time travel. Who thinks of changing the past rather than changing himself when he has a problem?"

"He has hardened memory. He will remember this version of events when he becomes real, but I have to die before he can become real. That is my penance. I suffer, I die to myself, and then I am renewed and reborn in a parallel timeline where my sins never took place. They are blotted out of all history books. All I have to do is die."

"You are crazy. I don't believe you."

"I am not paying you to believe me. Will you take the case? Because, if you don't—for the love of God, man! The Time Wardens gave her to me! Just like you'd give someone a pet cat! They'll just give her to someone else if I keep away from her, and I cannot keep away from her anyway. The temptation, it's too much! It's like a sickness. So you know what will happen if you allow me to live. Look, even if you don't believe me, will you take the case for her sake?"

I have to admit that I sat there thinking and scowling at him for a moment or two. Out of habit, I reached under the drawer where I keep my spare cigarettes, and was surprised to feel something meet my fingers. As soon as I touched it, I felt the tinkle of mist around my hand, and I remembered spending yesterday reading a memo to myself, from a version of myself who I was pretty sure did not exist and never would.

Look, I have my principles. I never take cases from Time Wardens, and I don't help time travelers kill themselves. Never.

Except this time I would.

I stood up. "All right."

Because I could swap cigarettes with nearly anyone in this quarter of the city, and get nearly anything I needed. Ammo, food, booze. A big breakfast and a square dinner.

He stood up. He looked me in the eye. He must have known exactly what I was thinking. "It seems you are no better than me, who uses women for sex, and no better than your friend who eats men for food. I am just a meal to you."

I sighed. "Well, since you put it that way, and since you are planning on erasing your memory tomorrow–"

And I hit him in the face hard enough to knock him backward over the chair and onto the floor.

## PROLOGUE TO A NEW BEGINNING.

Memo to Myself

*Written in Eternity, sent to the date Day Three Thousand And Twenty-Six Personal Subjective Time.*

I am leaving these papers under the bottom drawer rather than taking your pack of cigarettes.

About this time tomorrow, a man destined to be a Time Warden is going to hire you to kill himself via time paradox, or that is what it looks like. Looks can be deceiving.

He is going to tell you a fairy tale about a city that is Beyond the City Beyond Time, a City of Emerald Towers whose spires soar above a green world or gardens and arbors and forest rather than above any emptiness of mist.

He is telling the truth. He kills himself, but he does not really die. There is a real version of him that comes from a timeline where time travel is only used to cure past crimes, not to get away with them. That timeline leads to a city, this city, where the Proctors do not kill people except as an act of voluntary punishment, after which they are brought to life again as new people, people whose sins are only memories of events that never really happened.

That is what you really are, Jacob. You are not an assassin. They— the fallen Masters of Eternity—they twisted your past and tried to make you into something you are not. They changed this city of paradise into a Valhalla, and sent back agents to choose among the dead for historical figures to people their museum and amuse them. That includes their old bosses and old coworkers. Hardened memory does not remember anything for you if the whole time before you were ever born is changed. But they could not change you.

That is where your sense of justice comes from, your willingness to listen to people confess their wrongdoings to you, your willingness to take people as they are without passing judgment.

So go ahead and take the case. Punch him in the eye if you want, but take the damned case. When his alternate version becomes real here, he will be unfallen and forgiven, a pilgrim rather than a mere traveler through time.

As will you. As will we all.

—Yours, Jacob Quirinus Christoforo Frontino, S.J.
Tower of Final Forgiveness,
Transmetachronopolis

P.S.
Make sure I come into existence, Jake. Don't screw this one up.

## CASTALIA HOUSE

**SCIENCE FICTION**

*The End of the World as We Knew It* by Nick Cole
*CTRL-ALT REVOLT!* by Nick Cole
*Somewhither* by John C. Wright
*Back From the Dead* by Rolf Nelson
*Victoria: A Novel of Fourth Generation War* by Thomas Hobbes

**MILITARY SCIENCE FICTION**

*Starship Liberator* by David VanDyke and B. V. Larson
*The Eden Plague* by David VanDyke
*Reaper's Run* by David VanDyke
*Skull's Shadows* by David VanDyke
*There Will Be War Volumes I and II* ed. Jerry Pournelle

**FANTASY**

*Summa Elvetica* by Vox Day
*A Throne of Bones* by Vox Day
*The Green Knight's Squire* by John C. Wright
*Iron Chamber of Memory* by John C. Wright
*Awake in the Night* by John C. Wright

**FICTION**

*Brings the Lightning* by Peter Grant
*The Missionaries* by Owen Stanley
*An Equation of Almost Infinite Complexity* by J. Mulrooney
*Six Expressions of Death* by Mojo Mori

**NON-FICTION**

*Collected Columns, Vol. I: Innocence & Intellect, 2001—2005* by Vox Day
*Clio and Me* by Martin van Creveld
*MAGA Mindset: Making YOU and America Great Again* by Mike Cernovich
*SJWs Always Lie* by Vox Day
*Cuckservative* by John Red Eagle and Vox Day
*Equality: The Impossible Quest* by Martin van Creveld
*A History of Strategy* by Martin van Creveld
*4th Generation Warfare Handbook*
        by William S. Lind and LtCol Gregory A. Thiele, USMC
*Compost Everything* by David the Good
*Grow or Die* by David the Good

**AUDIOBOOKS**

*A History of Strategy* narrated by Jon Mollison
*Cuckservative* narrated by Thomas Landon
*Four Generations of Modern War* narrated by William S. Lind
*Grow or Die* narrated by David the Good
*Extreme Composting* narrated by David the Good
*A Magic Broken* narrated by Nick Afka Thomas

CPSIA information can be obtained
at www.ICGtesting.com
Printed in the USA
BVHW031419240820
587131BV00001B/171

9 789527 065235